ATROCITY

THE HAUNTING OF MORAVIAN VILLAGE

NEIL SATER

WEST KILBRIDE LLC

Cover Design by James, GoOnWrite.com

Library of Congress Control Number: 2025906975

ISBN: 979-8-9885508-4-6

Published by: West Kilbride LLC 6618 Morningside Dr. Cleveland OH 44141

First edition - 2025

Sign up for Neil Sater's newsletter through his website:

https://authorsater.com/

For Mom, who has always been there for me.
You're probably not a big fan of the front cover,
but you know me.

CONTENTS

Chapter 1

I've often wondered how things would have turned out if we hadn't been on magic mushrooms that night. Like, if we'd been thinking straight, my best friend might still be alive.

Just so you know, the shrooms were Karl's idea. I was kind of leery about this drug experiment. Until then, our usage had been limited to pot (plenty of it) and a bit of drinking. I went along with the plan, though. That was the thing about me and Karl: our corruption went both ways. The bad influence was a team effort, you might say.

For the record, it's not like either of us was experimenting with drugs because we had self-destructive tendencies or needed to escape from horrible lives or anything like that. We were just bored, that's all. Sixteen-year-old rebels chasing after cheap recreation. Stupid, I know.

So yeah, we were tripping that night in March of 1983. In fact, we were experiencing peak psychedelic effects when it all went down, making the whole incident even more mind-blowing. Except, in a way, the mushrooms might have dulled the weirdness of it, too...if that makes any sense. What I mean is, without being so high, I might not have been able to handle what was about to go down.

We spent the night at Karl's grandpa's house when it happened. He lived in a mobile home at the dead end of a gravel road in the southeastern corner of Homer County, outside a town called Moravian Village. Strange name, I know. I wonder where it came from. Moravian Village was nice but small, making my town of Clarkton seem like a sprawling metropolis.

Anyway, the house backed up to a farm field that ended at a narrow stretch of woods growing along the riverbank. Karl had campfires right along that tree line.

Being early March in Ohio, it wasn't exactly warm, but it wasn't so cold that we'd freeze sleeping in our tent. So that was our grand plan for keeping clear of his grandfather while we tripped.

We headed out before dark. After dropping our gear,

Karl lit a cigarette. I bummed one off him too. During our smoke break, we wandered into that band of woods. Karl let out a single word: "Damn!"

I added, "Holy crap."

The river was still swollen from a big rainstorm earlier in the week, and the water level was so high the trunks of most of the trees growing on the bank were underwater.

It suddenly dawned on me we were standing on a muddy slope, one slip from being swallowed by the current and swept away for good. I carefully stepped back from the bank to avoid losing my footing. Karl must've had the same realization because he did the same.

When we'd reached flat ground, I asked him, "Does it ever creep you out camping so close to that cemetery?"

Karl said, "Nah. Ghosts don't cross the river."

That seemed like wishful thinking, but I shrugged and let it go.

The river was sixty yards wide. A stone wall stretched along the opposite bank. The village cemetery sat on the other side, with the river bending into it right there. Beyond the graveyard was a row of homes, then the little town square of Moravian Village, a couple blocks off in the distance.

We finished our smokes and returned to the campsite. Once the fire got going, we set up the tent and laid out the two tarps on either side of the fire.

Karl dropped to his knees and pulled out the little baggie of shrooms, doing his best to divide them equally. Sitting cross-legged by the fire, we sucked and gnawed on the small pieces. I recall wondering if we were eating the right amount. Would it be enough to get a good buzz on? Or worse yet, would it be too much, and I'd lose my shit? There was no way to know.

The mushrooms were dry and chewy, so we washed them down with little swigs of the whiskey Karl swiped from his grandfather's stash. His grandpa, whom he called "Grand-Bob," was a total alky, so we weren't particularly worried he'd discover it had gone missing. Hell, Grand-Bob might have encouraged us to take it, for that matter. An old-timer like him would *not* have been cool with the mushrooms, though.

The fire was roaring by the time we felt that warm tipsiness from the whiskey, and it wasn't long before the shrooms kicked in.

We stretched out on our sides, each propped on an elbow. At first, it wasn't exactly comfortable, but as the drug's relaxing effects took hold, it became downright cozy.

The first sign of trouble, which I pretty much missed at the time, happened well after sunset, while we were peaking. Karl had told me about how he dorked out at school talking to the hot Cindy Barrett, and the more we dwelled on what he said to her, the funnier it got. My side hurt so bad from all the laughter, I started wondering if I was giving myself a hernia or something.

Some tiny rational part of my brain heard a splashing noise coming from the river. Only it didn't completely register, so I never mentioned it to Karl. Maybe I figured it was a muskrat or a mink. I just sort of thought, *That's strange,* and quickly pivoted back to the hilarious Cindy Barrett story, forgetting all about the sound.

Sometime later, I heard it again. I stopped laughing and held up my hand in the "halt" sign.

Karl gave me a dirty look, like annoyed at me for being a buzzkill.

Tilting my head back, I could make out nothing except the dark shapes of trees lining the river, silhouetted by the town's lights in the background, beyond the cemetery. From our position, I couldn't quite see the surface of the flooded river. If I'd gotten up, I would've had a full view, but that must've seemed like too much effort. If I had walked ten feet, I could have grabbed the flashlight beside the tent, but that would have taken even more energy.

I said, "I thought I heard something."

Karl just laughed and blurted out, "You're wasted, man!"

Which was totally true, so that got us rolling again, harder than ever.

You need to understand my state of mind. The fire looked beautiful, its vibrant colors enhanced by the psychedelic effects of the mushrooms. The warmth it cast was like ecstasy, so my body felt completely relaxed. Everything we talked about was so damn funny. I couldn't even conceive of anything disrupting our perfect little party night.

Until it did.

I heard a few footfalls off in the distance. I realize now this makes no sense, but I just kind of ignored them. Maybe because they were so soft, I didn't perceive them to be a threat. Or maybe I was so engrossed in our cheerful, stoned bubble that I refused to pay attention to anything else. They grew louder, though, and a little alarm in my brain started going off.

Karl carried on busting a gut, but I'd already forgotten what he was laughing about, and all my wonderful feelings began slipping away.

I turned toward the river and squinted into the darkness. At first, I saw nothing, but the footfalls were getting louder, and with them, there was a sloshing sound.

I gasped when a smudgy form emerged from the shadows. I stared, my eyes stretching wider as the shape came closer. Had the figure swum across the river? I thought about how swollen it was and told myself, *It can't be. Just ignore it.* I don't know, maybe this was some sort of coping mechanism. Anyhow, I couldn't ignore it, because it was *definitely* heading our way.

Karl was still giggling, totally clueless. Part of me wanted to scream and hightail it, but another part thought I needed to keep cool to avoid causing a bad reaction from this stranger. Can't make the situation worse by overreacting, right? Looking back now, that's exactly what I should have done.

Karl flinched when the stranger stepped up to the fire, stopping just a few feet from Karl's head. You can imagine how jarring it was for him. I had some advanced warning, but not Karl. Suddenly, there's an intruder barging into our happy little world.

Next, for me, came the shock of this thing's appearance.

The firelight reflected off his skin, which was tinted an odd shade of gray. He wasn't dressed for the weather at all. His arms were exposed, and I'd never seen such scrawny twigs. He looked like one of the starving Cambodian kids they used to show in those charity fundraising commercials. Something was hanging from his neck. After a while, I realized it was a turtle shell, about the size of a fist. Another thing I noticed was his ratty shoes. You couldn't really call them that, though. They were more like scraps of leather wrapped around his feet.

He just stood there. There was no *hello*, *excuse me*, or anything like that.

Karl tilted his head back, clearing the bill of his baseball cap from his line of sight, and stared up with eyes as wide as beer mugs, like questioning if it was all just a hallucination. I *wished* I was just seeing things, but the shock of it all jolted me into a more sober state, so I *knew* this was real.

An ember popped, interrupting the silence surrounding the campfire. That seemed to shake Karl out of his stupor. He asked, "Who are you?"

I remember thinking that was a strange question, but I'm sure Karl was wigging out.

"I am Thomas," the stranger said, his voice all gravelly. He stepped toward Karl, crouched, and reached so close that all Karl needed to do was lift his hand a few inches, and they could shake. Karl kind of melted away at first, then recovered, and reluctantly held up his hand.

While the two of them shook, I noticed how close Thomas—might as well call him that, since he said this was his name—was standing to the fire. His pants were made of some heavy cloth material, wet and ragged, ending above the ankles, making them into what we'd call "highwaters." Within seconds, steam poured off those tattered pant legs. The heat on his exposed ankles should have caused him to jump away, but he didn't. I swear, I caught a whiff of burning meat, and it made me want to ralph.

Before I knew it, Thomas was turning to me. I got my first good look at his face. He looked younger than us, maybe thirteen years old. His cheekbones protruded from his gaunt face, and his stringy black hair clung to his forehead.

What really flipped me out, though, were his eyes. They had no shine to them. They were dull and shriveled, but the color...oh, my God...they had a reddish glow, like when someone takes a drag on a cigarette at night. I had to look away.

With his hand coming at me, he said it again. "I am Thomas." I wanted to scoot backward, but managed to hold my ground, feeling like I had to avoid offending him. I realize that makes no sense—but that's how I felt.

He stepped between me and the fire, blocking the heat and casting shadows over me. Fighting my urge to roll away, I slowly stuck out my hand. He grasped it and squeezed. His hand was wet, but that didn't exactly surprise me. What caught me off guard was how cold it was, completely lacking any hint of warmth. Like I was gripping a ham hock that had been dunked in a bucket of ice water.

One more time, he said, "I am Thomas."

Okay, we know, I thought. Then, I realized we hadn't told him our names. We hadn't said anything, for that matter.

"I'm Sean," I said, still trapped in the grossest handshake imaginable. "That's my friend, Karl."

I pulled my hand away from his cold grip, feeling gritty residue, which I went about wiping away.

Thomas stepped aside, and the warmth from the fire returned.

Karl asked him where he came from. It was the question I wanted to ask, but hadn't dared.

Thomas pointed into the darkness, toward the river.

That's when I saw the back of his head. A wide gap in his hair exposed a mess of scars and scabs, running from the crown of his head to the base of his skull. Like an injury that had been trying to heal over, but couldn't quite get there. I almost puked at the sight, but fought off my gag reflex.

Karl was looking in the direction where Thomas had pointed, so he totally missed what I was taking in. But based on our positions relative to the firelight, I was the only one who could have seen the grotesque wound, anyway.

Karl turned back to the fire. If he had seen what I had, he would never have done what came next. He held up the whiskey bottle and asked, "Want a hit?"

No way, man! I wanted to scream. But I kept my mouth shut.

That's one thing that always drove me crazy about Karl. He seemed to want to make friends with everyone. I'm not that way at all. But even with Karl being a social butterfly, I'm pretty sure he wouldn't have invited this freak to join us if he had seen what I'd seen. Unfortunately, he *didn't* see it.

Thomas dropped to the bare ground between our tarps and squirmed into a cross-legged sitting position. He was so close to the fire the knees of his pants began steaming within seconds. Except it didn't seem to bother him.

Karl unscrewed the cap and handed over the open bottle.

My eyes were glued to Thomas. He peeked into the bottle, then took a swig. He swallowed without wincing at the alcohol burn...like he was Grand-Bob or something.

Karl picked up his pack of cigarettes and tapped one out. He had this red Winston lighter that was his pride and joy. I admit, it was pretty cool. When you squeezed down the chrome lever on top, it would light, and when you let go, a little cap would snap over the flame, putting it out.

Karl lit his smoke, and I noticed Thomas watching him. When Karl put that lighter down on the corner of his tarp, Thomas couldn't take his awful red eyes off it.

I stared into the fire's embers, my fried mind scrambling for some way to escape. Karl wasn't going to be any help. It would have been a different story if he'd been onto the fact that this monstrosity had come from across the river, or if he'd seen the gruesome wound on the backside of its head. But my friend was oblivious on both accounts. He was stuck in happy-land.

Movement caught my eye, and I saw Thomas tuck something into his waistband. It looked like a small leather pouch, but I had no idea what it was.

The next thing I remember was Thomas holding the bottle out to me. All I could think was how his shriveled lips had been on it. I waved it off and shook my head.

Thomas swung his arm over to Karl.

When Karl took the bottle, I tried to catch his attention. The campfire light made it hard to see, so I wasn't sure if I'd made eye contact with him. I gave him one of those quick head shakes to warn him. Karl didn't take a drink, so I figured he'd seen me.

I started spacing out again. But before I knew it, Karl was tipping the bottle back. A few seconds later, he spat it out, spraying the fire with a mouthful of whiskey. The alcohol half sputtered and half ignited when it hit the embers, exploding steam and flames into the air.

Karl shot upright and went into a spitting fit, like when you get a mouthful of something gross and you have to work it all out. He yelled at Thomas, "What the hell was that?" Karl clearly thought Thomas had put something in the bottle. He was *so* pissed. I knew he wasn't going to let it go.

Thomas just glared at Karl.

I wasn't sure if Thomas had done something to the whiskey. I'd been spacing out, my eyes aimed at the campfire, my attention tangled up in my troubled thoughts. But obviously, Karl was convinced. Later, I'd come around. Now, I'm sure that little leather pouch had something to do with it.

Karl climbed to his feet while making tiny, rapid-fire spits. He hovered over Thomas like he was going to kick his ass. But Thomas was unfazed. He just stared into the fire, looking like he was daydreaming.

This was when I decided I needed to get us the hell out of there. A graceful exit was no longer necessary. I started to stand, saying, “C’mon, Karl.”

When I pulled myself up, I almost toppled over. My legs had fallen asleep, but I hadn’t realized it. I said, “Let’s go,” even though I struggled to keep myself upright.

I knew how warped it was facing Grand-Bob while tripping, but we had no choice. We just had to get away from Thomas. So, I staggered around the fire on feet I couldn’t feel, grabbed Karl by the shoulders, and pulled him away. He didn’t resist much, mostly because he was still focused on clearing his mouth.

I remember questioning whether we should grab our stuff, but quickly dismissed the idea. It wasn’t worth slowing us down.

I yanked Karl around and pushed him away from the fire, steering him toward the house.

We started to book it across the field. But really, it was tough to move quickly. We were high and had to step around the field furrows and last year’s corn crop stubble. Plus, I had pins and needles in my legs.

I couldn’t shake the feeling that Thomas was coming after us, so before long, I looked over my shoulder.

> There he was, still sitting at the fire, acting as if he belonged there.
>
> The further we got across the field, the more relief I felt that we'd gotten away from this creep, whatever he was.
>
> Little did I know, the damage was already done.

Heather Warner sucked in a deep breath and held it as she leaned back in her chair. She stared at the slowly moving cassette tape wheels and listened for more of the teenage boy's voice. Only the soft white noise of the tape's blank tail was audible.

After a minute or two, she pressed the Fast-Forward button and counted ten Mississippis before resuming Play. All she heard was more of the blank tape hum. She advanced through the remainder and ejected the cartridge when it reached the end.

With pursed lips, Heather studied the handwritten label, written in the distinct style of her mother's printing: "Sean Davidson – January 7, 1984." After a moment of hesitation, she flipped the cassette over to the B side, slid it into the player, and pushed Play.

Her mother's voice came through the speakers. "Okay, it's recording. This is Sean Davidson's story, continued. Go ahead, Sean."

Chapter 2

We ran across the field for a while, but eventually, I had to stop and catch my breath. Karl held up, too. He was a more serious smoker than I was, so he was huffing and puffing even harder than me.

I didn't want to turn around, but I felt like I had to make sure Thomas wasn't coming after us, so I did.

When I looked across the field, nobody was near the fire. I stared hard at the trees. With the cloud cover, there wasn't much moonlight. I mostly looked for movement in the shadows, but didn't see any.

Karl said, "What the fuck?"

I just stood there, shaking my head. What could I say? I kept looking along the riverbank. The freak had vanished.

My brain was still buzzed, but all the fun had gone out of it. I asked Karl what we'd do now.

He glared at the area we'd just left and said, "We're not going back out there."

I was totally down with that.

We turned toward Grand-Bob's house, now a stone's throw away. We just stood there for a while, watching the TV light flickering through the gap between the drapes. Seeing that always gave me a weird feeling, but my frazzled mind jacked up the freakiness of it.

Karl started trudging toward the house. I sighed and followed. Where else were we going to go?

We tried to enter quietly, but as it turned out, there was nothing to worry about. Grand-Bob was passed out in his recliner. In the dark, the TV threw creepy shadows on the walls. An empty bottle of Southern Comfort sat on the floor by his chair. I didn't see a glass.

Karl turned off the TV, and we headed toward his bedroom.

After he shut the door behind us, Karl looked me in the eye. "That sonofabitch put something in the bottle...something slimy. And gritty...it tasted like shit."

I had to try hard to focus on what he said, but I kept thinking, *That's not the worst of it.* I said, "He came from across the river."

Karl twisted his face into that *you're full of crap* expression.

"I kid you not. I heard sloshing. And I saw him coming at us from the bank."

Karl propped himself against the edge of his bed and stared at the floor, like trying to picture how anything could have made it across that flooded river.

"You couldn't see it, but the back of his head..." I tried to find the right words. "It was...all...torn up."

He looked at me cockeyed.

"It was a nasty wound, but not..." I bared my teeth in a grimace. "...not fresh."

Karl slowly shook his head, saying, "What the hell?"

You can say that again, I kept thinking. *What the hell?*

With the night ruined, we didn't stay up much later. Karl dug an old comforter from the closet, which we spread out on the floor at the foot of his bed, my poor man's mattress. It wasn't the most comfortable bed, but that wasn't why I got such a crappy night's sleep. The problem was, I couldn't get Thomas out of my head.

At one point, I dreamed we were out at the fire, and Thomas began moaning. He started out quiet but kept getting louder until I came to my senses and realized I was dreaming. The moaning, that was Karl.

I sat up in the darkness and said, "Hey, Karl!"

He kept on moaning.

I patted the top of the bed until I felt Karl's feet, covered with blankets, and gave him a good shake.

Karl snorted himself awake. He groaned and said, "What?"

I told him he was moaning. I thought about cracking some joke about him having a wet dream starring Cindy Barrett, but my own dreams had spoiled the mood.

The shadows shifted as he rolled over, and he said, "My arms hurt."

I laid back down and pulled the blanket over me.

I wonder now if I had gotten up and taken a look, would things have turned out any different?

The sound of Grand-Bob hacking up a lung in the bathroom across the hall woke me up. I peeled my eyes open and blinked. It was after sunrise, but cloudy, so gray light filtered in through the curtains.

Staring at the water stains on the ceiling, I thought about the night before. In the daylight, it seemed distant, less threatening.

I sat up and stretched, looking over at Karl, buried under the blankets, not making a sound.

Grand-Bob pissing in the toilet broke the silence. The walls in his mobile home were so thin, it sounded like he could have been right there in the room with us.

I pulled myself up and stood, rubbed the sleep from my face, and went over to the window to peek out the grimy pane. Across the field, a buzzard circled over the stand of trees lining the river. The flap of our tent fluttered in the breeze. That bird and the tent flap were the only signs of movement.

When the toilet flushed, I dropped the curtain and turned toward Karl. He was lying on his side with one arm wrapped around his head. I blinked and leaned closer. A rash had spread over his wrist.

I called his name. My throat felt tight, so it came out like a croak.

He didn't move.

My heart began beating fast. Was he even breathing? Louder this time, I said, "Hey, Karl?"

He still didn't move.

I reached out and grabbed his shoulder through the blanket. It felt warm, which I remember being relieved by. I shook him and called his name.

He let out a moan.

I wondered if this might be an aftereffect of the mushrooms. Like he was...I don't know, hungover?

Except I wasn't, so that made no sense. Plus, he had that rash. I looked at my arms. They looked normal. Rubbing my hand over them, they felt normal.

I shook Karl harder this time and told him to wake

up.

He just kept on moaning, with a sick gurgle to it.

I leaned in and took a good look at the rash. The closer I got, the more painful it looked. Red stripes, blistered, like welts.

That's when I decided to get Grand-Bob. I pulled on my jeans and opened the door, just as Grand-Bob stepped out of the bathroom across the hall. Speaking of hangovers, I could immediately tell his was a doozy. He pulled his head upright and seemed to be straining to look in my direction.

"Morning," he said, then cleared his throat. "You slept inside?"

I scrambled for a story and told him we'd gotten cold.

"Mmmm," he replied and left it at that, turning to leave.

I hooked my thumb in the direction of the open doorway and told him I thought something might be wrong with Karl.

Grand-Bob stopped, turned back in my direction, leaned forward, and peered at him. His reek of alcohol just about knocked me over. He said, "That kid's a late sleeper. Deep sleeper too."

I shook my head and said, "Yeah, I know. Not like this, though. He was moaning a minute ago. And he's got some weird rash."

Grand-Bob tottered like he might still be drunk, then righted himself and stepped around me. While I followed him to the side of the bed, it came back to me about how Karl had said his arms hurt during the night. For a second, I questioned whether I had dreamed it, but I quickly realized I hadn't.

Grand-Bob shook him with both hands, saying, "Rise and shine, Buttercup."

Karl moaned again.

I wondered whether this could be some type of brain damage from the mushrooms, but I tossed that idea away. It hadn't happened to me, and I had pretty much the same amount as Karl.

Grand-Bob asked, "Something wrong, son?" He yanked the bedcovers down, exposing Karl's shoulder. Grand-Bob yelped and stepped back.

That same nasty rash covered Karl's shoulder, reaching halfway to his elbow. We both just stood there, shocked at the red discoloration on Karl's skin. The brightest splotches ran in wavy lines, crisscrossing over each other.

It was Grand-Bob who moved first. He crawled up on the bed and, from his knees, hoisted Karl into a sitting position. The bedcovers fell into Karl's lap, exposing his chest. The rash had spread there, too.

Karl's eyelids flickered, and he kind of whimpered like a dog. He slowly pried his eyes open and blinked. I could tell he was trying to sort out where he was. His eyes shifted around, and his head wobbled a few times before he caught hold of his bearings. He looked at me and I gave him a half-assed smile. As if I could smile us back to normal. He managed to return the smile, and I took that as a good sign.

Grand-Bob asked him if he was alright.

Karl turned his head toward him and nodded with a dazed look. He didn't look alright, but at least he was responding.

Grand-Bob pulled the bedcovers away and said, "Let's get you up, son." Karl slept in just his underwear, so I could see there was no rash on his legs.

After Grand-Bob crawled back off the bed, he motioned for me to give him a hand. I wanted to help, but I wasn't sure what the plan was, so I mostly just stood there, trying not to look useless.

Grand-Bob slid Karl's legs over to the edge of the mattress. Karl seemed to catch onto the idea, and he nudged forward until he sat on the side of the bed. With Grand-Bob and I on either side of him, we pulled him onto his feet. I couldn't help but try to avoid touching his rash, worried I might catch it.

Karl said, "I have to pee." He sounded like his mouth was full of nuts and bolts.

I said, "You're on your own for that, man."

Karl gave one of those little *ha* reactions, and I felt relieved. He sucked in a breath and then took a small step forward on his own power. After a couple more paces, I started telling myself maybe he was alright. But when he entered the hallway, he collapsed.

We rushed over, sidestepping the puddle of pee spreading around him, and Grand-Bob told me we needed to get him to the hospital.

I started to argue, but I caught myself and shut my mouth. You have to understand, part of me still thought this might have something to do with the mushrooms, so I needed to keep us out of trouble.

I didn't have any other plan, though. I guess I was

hoping all this might magically go away.

Karl had fallen face down, so when I reached the hallway, I got a full view of his upper back, covered with the same sick, squiggly lines. Grand-Bob was right: we needed to get him to the hospital.

Karl's grandma had spent her last couple of years in a wheelchair, so Grand-Bob went to fetch that from the closet by the front door. We hauled Karl up from the floor, wrapped him in the comforter from his bed, and seated him in the wheelchair.

I asked Karl if he was okay.

He nodded, but his unfocused eyes told me he wasn't. I felt stupid for having asked.

Grand-Bob had lost his license for driving drunk one too many times, so I drove. He sat in the back seat of my rust-bucket Ford Granada, holding Karl upright against him. I assumed we'd be heading to the Homer County Hospital in Clarkton, but Grand-Bob insisted we take him to Tri-County Hospital, which was in the opposite direction. I'd never even heard of it, but he said it was closer.

Between giving me directions, Grand-Bob spoke to Karl. With the hole in my muffler, I couldn't hear what he was saying, but I heard Karl mumble a few times. That encouraged me.

Along the way, Grand-Bob rolled the window down a crack and lit a smoke. I was glad since it covered up the smell of Karl's piss. My hands were shaking, which I couldn't tell was my nerves or my own craving for a cigarette. I always made a point of not smoking around adults who knew me. I might've broken that rule, but I didn't have any. Karl had left his pack—*and* his treasured lighter, I realized then—out by the campfire.

It was early on a Sunday, so the country roads were practically empty. I floored it, and we got there in less than half an hour. When I first saw the small building, I questioned whether it could be a hospital, but the letters on the top of the building spelled out TRI-COUNTY HOSPITAL.

I parked right at the Emergency Room entrance and snagged a hospital wheelchair from the vestibule. As I wheeled Karl to the reception desk, Grand-Bob yelled, "Something's wrong with my grandson!"

The waiting room was empty, so they admitted him right away. It soon became clear I could answer more of the questions than Grand-Bob could, so I took over while he parked the car and used the payphone to call Karl's parents.

When I pushed Karl into the ER wing, the nurse asked me how we were related.

A rare moment of genius struck me, and I told her he was my brother. Without that lie, they'd have told me to wait outside.

She gave me a long, doubtful look.

I realized she was probably wondering why we appeared about the same age, so I told her we were twins. I added, "Fraternal…obviously."

I don't know if she bought it, but she let it go.

When we got to the room, I helped her move Karl onto the exam table. I felt like I needed to explain why he smelled like pee, so I told her he wet himself when he collapsed.

She nodded like she didn't care about that and turned to Karl, asking him how he felt.

He tilted his head back, and with his eyes mostly closed and his mouth hanging open, he gave a little grunt. Then his chin dropped to his chest.

She held up a hospital gown and said, "Let's put this on you." But she froze when she removed the blanket we had wrapped him in. The longer she gawked at his chest, the more she frowned. The rash had gotten worse. It had also spread up his neck and down to his stomach.

She slipped each arm into the gown and asked me when the rash started.

I said, "Overnight, I think."

"Was he exposed to anything unusual?"

The whole Thomas thing was as unusual as hell, but my instinct was still to act cagey, so I shrugged. "Not that I know of."

"Has he ingested anything out of the ordinary?"

I shook my head a bit too quickly, and then a small part of me wondered if I should come clean about the mushrooms. I didn't, though. Looking back now, I was so focused on covering up the stupid shrooms that I never wondered if his last swig from the liquor bottle—and whatever was in that little leather pouch—had played a role. Anyway, it probably wouldn't have made any difference. By that point, it was most likely too late, no matter what.

She put on a pair of exam gloves and reclined Karl on the table. He closed his eyes completely. After opening one side of the gown, she tilted forward for a closer look. She placed her fingers from both hands on his chest and pulled the skin taut.

That's when I saw a ripple on his chest. I don't know how else to describe it. The previous summer, we had moles in the backyard. One day I was mowing the lawn, and I saw one moving around, just under the sod layer. A mound slid across the grass as the little bastard traveled along its tunnel. Karl's chest was like that.

The nurse must've seen it too, because she flinched.

"What was that?" I asked, leaning in while she leaned away.

Right then, the door swung open, and Grand-Bob stuck his head in, nodding when he saw he had the right room. He said, "Karl's parents are on their way," and handed me my keys.

The nurse pulled off her exam gloves, tossed them into the nearby garbage can, and headed straight for the door. I tried catching eye contact with her, but she was making every effort to avoid looking at me.

The last thing she said before escaping into the hall was, "The doctor will be in soon."

Chapter 3

Grand-Bob headed to the corner and plopped into the only chair, looking like he'd been beaten up.

My head felt numb. I asked myself, *What just happened?* No matter how I looked at it, it seemed clear something flipped that nurse out. Grand-Bob didn't seem bothered by her reaction, but he came in midway through it. I didn't say anything to him about what I'd seen. Why rile him up over something I couldn't explain? Anyway, I was counting on the doctor to get everything sorted out.

All we could do was wait. And we waited, alright.

When I was little, I stepped on a rusty nail sticking up from a swimming dock with a bare foot. We were on vacation in the middle of nowhere, Michigan. No hospital was nearby, so my dad took me to a rural clinic. It turned out the doctor was out on a house call, if you can believe that. We waited forever for him—at least it seemed that way to me and my painful foot. My dad kept my mind busy by pointing out everything in the room and explaining what it was for.

Waiting in the room with Karl and Grand-Bob, I started feeling like that same scared little kid. I tried playing my dad's game of distraction with myself, inspecting everything in the room: the glass jar of cotton swabs, the needle disposal bin, the blood pressure cuff. None of those things kept my focus, though. I kept thinking about how the nurse reacted, and everything else, going back to Thomas at the fire. It was like I was living in a nightmare. I started feeling like I was going to puke. I forced myself to study the skeleton diagram on the wall, which did help take my mind off all the craziness just a little.

At least Karl seemed comfortable enough, sprawled out on that exam table, looking like he'd fallen asleep. After a while, Grand-Bob dozed off too, complete with his raucous snoring. I couldn't believe it.

I made a point of watching the clock, so I know it took over half an hour for the doctor to show up. When he finally popped in, the first thing I noticed was how young he looked.

"I'm Doctor Dwyer, the resident on duty."

I remember thinking, *Resident? Does that mean he's not even an actual doctor?*

Dr. Dwyer picked up the charts, looked them over, and asked, "This young man isn't doing so well?"

Grand-Bob, who had just woken up, cleared his throat. "You can say that again. It's like his head's gone to mush."

The doctor placed the chart on the counter and turned to Karl. He hesitated when he lifted Karl's gown, staring at the rash. I stared too, thinking about that tunneling mole thing.

He went back to the counter and pulled on a pair of exam gloves, then used his stethoscope to listen to Karl's breathing, or his heart, or both. Even with that cold metal disc pressing on his chest, Karl slept right through it.

Dr. Dwyer wheeled the stool over beside the exam table. He squatted on it, lifted Karl's arm, rolled back the gown's sleeve, and studied the rash. He rotated his arm and stared some more. Before we'd left the house, the rash was on Karl's wrists and shoulder, but now, two hours later, his entire arm was covered.

Grand-Bob asked, "Ever seen anything like that?"

The doctor crossed his arms and said, "Could be scabies."

I *knew* this was *not* scabies. I'm no doctor, but I happen to know a little something about scabies. In elementary school, there was a kid named Ronnie Hogan in our class. There must've been a dozen kids in the Hogan family, each spaced out by one year. Well, in fifth grade, the Hogan family had a scabies infestation, and every one of them got infected. By the time the school found out, it had already been spread to dozens of non-Hogans, some in every grade. And guess what? Yup, I was one of the lucky ones. So, I know what scabies are. They're little tiny vermin that burrow into your skin, munch away at the underlayment, have sex, lay eggs, crap, and die. Then, the eggs hatch, and there's even more going at it. Meanwhile, you're going out of your mind with the itch. Nice, huh?

Karl never let me live down catching scabies from Ronnie Hogan. Now, Karl had something even worse. No, this was *definitely* not scabies.

The doctor picked up Karl's arm again and ran his gloved hands along the back of the forearm, homing in on an open sore. I saw the skin ripple, right next to that hole.

The doctor said, "Hmmm," and spread the opening apart using both thumbs. There was no blood until he did that, but then the wound turned red the moment before it happened. I know how strange this sounds, but I saw it with my own two eyes: The end of a worm popped out of that bloody hole. It looked like an earthworm. It wriggled out half an inch or more, and the doctor scooted back, dropping Karl's arm. Then, the worm sucked itself back into the hole and was gone.

My brain got all gummed up with what I saw. I looked at Grand-Bob, but he was staring off into the void. At first, I figured maybe he was in shock, but then I realized he'd just been spacing out, so he missed it completely.

Dr. Dwyer suddenly seemed to have a fire lit under him. He stood up and began pulling off his latex gloves, saying, "I'm going to order a surgical exam. We'll need to have you move to the waiting area."

When Grand-Bob and I didn't move, the doctor said, "Can you find your way out, or do you need help?"

Grand-Bob snapped out of it and told him he knew the way. He put his hand on my back and steered me toward the door.

I took one last look at Karl before the door closed

behind us, and the sight of my best friend lying there almost made me cry. I fought off the tears, but I'll never shake that image of him looking so out of it, like he'd slipped into a coma.

And that worm. I swear, it looked like an earthworm. What the hell was that? And were there others? There was no way there wasn't.

When we walked into the waiting room, Grand-Bob told me he needed a smoke. He headed outside, and I dropped into one of the waiting room chairs.

I was facing the windows, so I got to watch Grand-Bob light his cigarette, which revved up my own cravings. My whole body felt jittery, and my throat was tightening up. My mind kept cycling through all the batshit things that had happened in the past half day, and it all seemed so unreal.

I barely noticed when a man and woman came running across the parking lot. Grand-Bob dropped his cigarette, stomped on it, and then wandered over to intercept the couple before they came bursting through the doorway. That's when I realized this frantic couple was Karl's parents.

I didn't want to talk with Mr. and Mrs. Wolf. They'd be full of questions, most of which I'd need to dodge. But I knew I had to face the music, so I got up and headed that way. I moved slowly, giving Grand-Bob a chance to fill them in.

When the automatic doors parted and the rush of cold air hit me, the three of them turned my way. I saw Mrs. Wolf's eyes were red from all the crying she'd been doing, and I lost it. I burst into tears, like the scared little boy I'd been trying to grow up from.

I covered my mouth with one palm and squeezed my eyes shut. When I blinked them back open, I saw Mrs. Wolf closing in on me. I wasn't expecting that, and for a second, I thought she might tackle me, like taking out her anger on me. It sounds totally mental now, but my guilty brain knew this had happened on my watch.

It turned out to be a hug she was serving up. She'd never hugged me before, so it caught me off guard. I just stood there feeling awkward, and I never even thought to hug her back.

When she pulled away, wiping her own cheeks dry with a balled-up tissue she had clenched in her fist, she asked me if I was okay.

I wasn't okay, but I nodded anyway. Then I said something dumb. I said, "But Karl's not." As if they didn't know already.

She began crying again and pulled me back in. This time, I returned the hug, blubbering along with her, her hair tickling my face. In hindsight, my crying might've saved me from the immediate interrogation, although that would come later.

Mr. Wolf asked Grand-Bob, "So, they said we need to wait in the waiting area?"

"Yeah," the old man answered. "Doc said someone would come get us when they're done."

"Done doing *what?*"

Grand-Bob scratched his head, then gave a wimpy shrug.

Mr. Wolf turned and headed straight for the door.

Mrs. Wolf let go of me. She dabbed her eyes with the tissue clump and then jogged after her husband.

Grand-Bob and I followed them inside, but hung back at the chairs closest to the entrance doors.

Karl's parents started picking on the desk lady, demanding to see their son. I'm sure they would've headed straight in if that door hadn't been locked. The desk lady was patient at first, but Mr. Wolf started getting hot.

Grand-Bob went over to try to calm him down, but Mrs. Wolf turned on him. She gave him a look that could kill. "Let us deal with this, Bob. You were supposed to be watching him!"

I thought Mr. Wolf might stick up for his father, but he didn't. He went right back at it with the desk lady, while Grand-Bob walked back to where I was sitting, looking like a whipped dog. I felt bad for him, but I admit part of me was relieved. Mrs. Wolf seemed to be blaming someone other than me.

When Mr. Wolf pounded his fist on the counter, the desk lady picked up her phone. "I need security," she said into the handset.

Mr. Wolf toned it down right away. I thought she might have been bluffing. I couldn't believe this hospital was big enough to have security. But within a minute, a chubby rent-a-cop barged through the doors. Within another minute, Karl's dad apologized, and they headed to the corner to join Grand-Bob and me.

Mr. and Mrs. Wolf couldn't seem to bring themselves to sit down, so they stood and took turns pacing around. I began watching the clock, which made it turn even slower.

We'd all look over each time the doors opened. It happened four or five times. Once, a janitor came out to clean the waiting room bathrooms. The other times, it was visitors leaving.

After an hour and a half, the doors swung open, and a nurse called, "The Wolf family?"

We all jumped up and went for the open doors. As the nurse led us down the hall, Mrs. Wolf asked her how Karl was doing.

She said, "I'm sorry, I don't know anything. The doctor will have an update."

When we turned the corner, I saw the resident standing beside the nurse's station, talking with another doctor, a white-haired man. Dr. Dwyer looked our way, and my chest seized at the sight of his pallbearer's expression. The nurse stepped to the side and let us continue on without her. I felt the walls closing in.

"Mr. and Mrs. Wolf, I'm Dr. Dwyer," he said as we approached. He didn't offer a handshake. "This is Dr. McCloskey, the attending physician."

Dr. McCloskey nodded, but his face had the same gloomy look. "Let's step into the break room." Dr. McCloskey pointed with his hand past the nurse's station.

Mr. Wolf asked, "Where's Karl?"

Dr. McCloskey pointed down the hall again, saying, "Let's talk in the break room."

"We need to see him," Mrs. Wolf said. "Where is he?"

I watched Dr. Dwyer's eyes turn to the room we were standing near, with a curtain pulled across the opening, and I knew then where Karl was.

My knees went weak. I grabbed the wooden banister mounted on the wall and leaned on it.

Dr. McCloskey seemed to give up on the break room. He cleared his throat and said, "Mr. and Mrs. Wolf, we did everything we could..."

That's when Karl's mom fainted.

Heather Warner leaned across the desk and tugged a tissue from the box. She dabbed the wetness from her eyes while allowing the tape to continue playing, emitting its barely audible hiss. After a while, the white noise ended, and the tape stopped turning. She clicked Stop.

With a sniffle, she slid a manila folder out from under the cassette player.

In her mother's print, "Sean Davidson" filled the folder's tab in blue marker. She rubbed a finger over her lips as she stared at the phone number in the top corner of the folder. She nodded, reached for the receiver, and dialed the number.

The other end rang once. Twice. Then three times. On the fourth ring, just as Heather started thinking she might not have to go through with it after all, a young man answered, "Hello?"

She froze.

He repeated, "Hello?"

Heather cleared her throat. "Hi, is this Sean Davidson?" She already knew it was, having recognized the voice from the recording.

A hesitation. "Yeah. Who's this?"

She pursed her lips and took in a deep breath through her nose. "My name's Heather Warner. I'm Marilyn Warner's daughter."

The line fell silent.

"Do you remember my mom?"

"Of course." Sean's voice sounded strained. "How is she?"

Heather swallowed. "She's dead."

After a long, uncomfortable stretch, Sean asked the inevitable question. "How?"

Heather squeezed her eyelids shut and pressed her hand against her forehead. "That's why I'm calling."

Sean waited.

"I've been digging through my mother's files. I learned about what happened to your friend Karl. It might have something to do with what happened to my mom."

Chapter 4

Sean pressed the Ford Granada's brakes as the first assemblage of headstones came into view. The road began its wide sweep, following the bend in the river. He turned into the entrance drive at the center of the arc and passed under an ornate iron arch, spelling out MORAVIAN VILLAGE CEMETERY.

Just beyond the arch was a row of empty parking spots. Sean backed into the first one but left the car idling. Say what you will about the Granada, but there was no complaining about the air conditioning, as long as Sean kept it topped off with Freon. He'd added a fresh can before hitting the road on this hot July day.

He pushed in the car's cigarette lighter and stared at the expanse of headstones in the distance, which stretched several football fields. The cemetery seemed bigger than anything Moravian Village could have ever needed. Who knows? Maybe this was the main cemetery for the whole eastern end of Homer County.

People are just dying to get buried there. Sean groaned at the thought of his father's favorite joke, which his dad would unfailingly recite each time he'd pass a graveyard. Judging by the endless rows of headstones, maybe it was true in this case.

The cigarette lighter popped out, startling him. He pulled a smoke from his pack of Winstons and pinched it between his lips.

With shaking hands, he pressed the glowing end of the car's lighter against the tip.

Why was he nervous? Sean took a long drag and thought it over. It was partly the unknown. What exactly was he stepping into here?

But it was more than that, he realized. This was where the whole thing with Karl had gone down, just across the river from here. He'd only been to Moravian Village once since Karl died, when he'd met Marilyn Warner. And now he was back. This time, to meet her daughter, Heather. At the *cemetery,* of all places. Why did she ask to meet him *here?*

He blew out a plume of smoke, opened the door, killed the engine, and climbed out into the heat.

There was no sign of Heather yet. Not surprisingly, seeing as he was fifteen minutes early. Good thing, too. Viewing the area where he'd spent that last evening with Karl...it would be best to take that in alone. Although he was now on the opposite side of the river, being here would bring new life to those emotions he'd worked for over a year to quell.

His throat tightened as he walked down the graveyard's driveway toward the river. He stopped at the street and looked both ways, just as his mother had taught him. This was completely unnecessary, though. No cars were in sight. Few probably ever came this way anyway, but if one did, he certainly would have heard it.

The heat poured off the asphalt as he crossed the roadway, his heart beating faster with each step. The opposite shoulder of the road butted up against a mortared stone wall, three feet high, a giant arc following the river bend for more than one hundred yards in either direction.

Directly across from the cemetery entrance and in front of the stone wall, a small grassy stretch filled the middle of the sweep. In the center stood a single park bench, with fresh mulch carpeting the ground underneath.

Sean walked past the bench and placed his hands on top of the hot stone wall. He stared across the river, consumed with thoughts of that night when he'd gazed over from the other side.

A thick row of cottonwood and sycamore trees lined the opposite bank. Small gaps in the leaf cover revealed a field of corn beyond. But from where Sean stood, none of the gaps in the leafed-out trees provided a view of Grand-Bob's mobile home. *It's out there, though,* Sean thought as a hollow ache wrenched inside his gut.

Sunshine glimmered on the water's surface at the bottom of a gravel-covered slope, a forty-foot drop below the wall. Clear and calm, the sixty-yard-wide river barely showed a current.

As Sean took another drag on his cigarette, he thought about how swollen the river had been that night, the water reaching halfway up the banks. It would have been impossible to swim across, yet Thomas had done just that. Sean peered over his shoulder at the cemetery. Where exactly had Thomas come from?

The sound of a car interrupted his train of thought. A white Chevy Chevette swung around the bend, slowing as it approached the cemetery entrance. Was this Heather? *Could be.* It was a teenage girl, at least. *A fine one, too.* It *had* to be her. How many teenage girls come to the cemetery alone?

Sean ground his cigarette butt into the side of the stone wall and dropped it in the nearby raccoon-proof trash bin, then headed back across the road. The Chevette turned into a parking space near his rusty Granada.

As he walked around his car, the Chevette door swung open, and the brown-haired girl stepped out, dressed for the hot day in a white halter top and jean shorts. "Sean?"

Sean lifted his chin, his attempt at a cool greeting. "Heather?"

When she nodded, he was pleased. She was pretty, alright, but not in a made-up way.

He guessed they were close in age, but she might've been a year younger. Two years, at the most. Since she was driving, she had to be at least sixteen.

"I thought I was going to be the early one," she said.

Say something funny, a small voice in Sean's mind implored him as he approached. But the best he could do was, "You drove in from Akron just now?"

"Yes. Fairlawn, to be exact. It's near Akron." She checked her watch. "Just under ninety minutes. How long was your drive?"

"Clarkton's not far. Less than half an hour on country roads."

Heather pulled an open can of 7 Up from the plastic cupholder hanging on the driver's door and tilted it back, draining it. "Want one?" She motioned to the red and white "Little Playmate" cooler on the passenger seat. "It's ice cold."

Sean bobbed his head as he considered this, which Heather seemed to take as a yes. She slid back into the driver's seat, reached over to flip open the cooler, and pulled out a can. Before he knew it, she had tossed it, and it was flying his way.

A flash of panic bloomed in Sean's mind. He pictured himself not making the catch, and this good-looking chick would know how unathletic he was within one minute of meeting him. But he surprised himself and snagged it solidly in both hands.

Attempting to make the whole thing look like second nature, he promptly snapped the tab, and 7 Up foam began spewing from the opening. *Of course, dumbass,* he said to himself as he pointed the can away from himself and the car. *Still ended up looking like a dork.*

Heather laughed, but the way she did it, it didn't come off like she was laughing *at* him. He laughed along with her before gulping some of the sweet, icy foam off the can.

As Heather climbed back out of the car, she said, "Thanks for meeting me." They made eye contact just long enough for Sean to notice her striking amber eye color.

The pop continued to fizz. He took another slurp, passing the can to his other hand, giving his flash-frozen fingertips a break. When he'd suctioned off the bulk of the froth, he said, "I'm glad you called. I'd been expecting to hear from your mother. I was starting to wonder..."

She gave a solemn nod and opened the Chevette's rear door, retrieving a leather portfolio from the back seat.

"I liked your mom a lot. I was so shocked when you told me she...passed away." He caught himself before the harsher word "died" slipped out.

Heather sighed. "It's still so hard to believe she's gone." She gazed off into the cemetery, the breeze blowing strands of hair into her face.

Sean froze, trying to work out if she had started to cry, but he couldn't see enough of her face to tell.

After a long moment, Heather brushed the hair away and spun around toward the river, motioning for him to follow.

As they made their way along the driveway, Sean tried to devise what he could say to break the awkward silence. He drew another blank, though.

"You guys were over there?" Heather asked when they closed in on the stone wall, pointing at the opposite side of the river.

Sean nodded and placed the sweating can of 7 Up on the wall. "Karl's grandfather lives across that cornfield beyond the trees."

Heather grinned. "What did you guys call him again?"

"Grand-Bob." Sean chuckled. "He's a character."

"He sure sounds like one. Does he still live there?"

"I'm sure he does. I haven't spoken with the Wolfs in the past year, though." He almost left it at that, then added, "I can't help but feel like they blame me."

Heather chewed on her lower lip for a spell. "Guilt haunts us after someone close to us dies. Trust me...I know the feeling."

Sean shuffled his feet and wiped the sweat from his forehead.

"My mom had a copy of Karl's autopsy report in her file. It says he died of an unclassified parasite."

Sean guffawed. "What bullshit. The coroner told us if he had died in one of the more populated counties, they might've been able to identify the parasite. Looked like earthworms to me." He waited for Heather to wrinkle her nose.

Without showing any gross-out reaction, Heather asked, "The Sheriff's Office investigated?"

"Yeah, two different deputies interviewed me. I never mentioned the mushrooms. I was worried the autopsy might find traces of that. Apparently, the Homer County coroner doesn't test for psilocybin either."

When Heather gave him a questioning look, he said, "That's the psychedelic compound in magic mushrooms."

"Did you tell them about Thomas?"

Sean blew a raspberry. "How could I? They would have questioned if we were on drugs, and, of course, we were." He paused and wiped his open hands down his face. "What happened...I can't prove anything, but I *know* that freak killed Karl. He put something in Karl's drink—something from that little leather pouch."

They stood in silence for a spell until Heather broke it. "So, what made you contact my mother?"

"It was her book."

Heather reached into the leather bag and pulled out a paperback, holding it up so he could see the cover.

Ohio Ghostly Road Trip

The Most Haunted Houses in Every County

"That's it. She profiled two haunted houses in this county. Homer County. So, I thought she might be interested in hearing what happened to Karl."

Heather rubbed her fingers across the cover. "Funny thing: more copies of this book sold in the first year than all her other books combined. But she wasn't exactly proud of it."

Sean cocked an eyebrow. "Why not?"

"She wanted to dig deeper into some of these legends. But the publisher had other ideas. So, when you wrote her that letter, she was all in."

"I was glad she took an interest. I hoped she could get to the bottom of what happened."

"Where did you meet her?"

Sean pointed toward the town square. "At the library. She had a meeting room reserved, and that's where she recorded me telling what happened with Karl."

A thought popped into Sean's head, triggering a twinge of dismay: Heather had listened to his tape. Had he said anything embarrassing? *Good chance of that,* he thought. He cracked his knuckles and tried to put it out of his mind.

"You got my mom started on her next project. She decided she'd found a new legend in the making, all centered right here." Heather raised her hand, palm facing skyward, and swept it from the river to the cemetery.

Sean tried to lick his lips, but his tongue felt like sandpaper. Was there any chance Heather was blaming him for her mother's death? She didn't seem to be, however. Maybe this was just his guilt about Karl, bleeding over. He took a swig from his 7 Up, which had already lost its chill and was going flat.

Heather placed the book back in the satchel, pulled out a cassette tape, and held it out for him. "I want you to listen to this."

Sean took it and stared at the name printed on the label: "Jackson McCarthy," followed by a date. He didn't recognize the name. "What is it?"

"Someone else's story," Heather said.

"There's someone else?"

"Seems that way. Let's see what you think."

Sean studied the handwritten date on the label as if it might tell him something. It read, "January 7, 1984." *Yeah,* he said to himself. *The same day she interviewed* me.

He placed the tape beside his 7 Up can and spun around to face Heather. "And what about your mother? Can I ask what happened?"

Heather sucked in a deep breath, stepped around the park bench, and took a seat at one end of it. Her shoulders slumped as she gazed across the street in the direction of the cemetery. "She drowned."

Sean's heart skipped a beat as he took the words in.

Heather stared ahead, blinking repeatedly while twirling her gold necklace between her fingers. A heart-shaped locket hung from the chain.

Sean waited for her to say more, but when she didn't, he cleared his throat and asked, "How? Where?"

"Right here," Heather pointed with her thumb, over her shoulder, at the river. "Right effing here."

"No way!" Sean picked up his pop and the cassette tape, walked around to the front of the park bench, and sat beside Heather, arranging the tape and the can on the bench slats between them. "I mean...she came *here?*"

Heather nodded. "It was four months ago." She paused and sniffed. "When she didn't come home, my dad called the sheriff. They found her car parked at the town square. The thing is, the cemetery closes at dusk, so she couldn't park here."

"She came at night?"

"Yeah."

Sean shivered with the thought. "Why?"

Heather tapped the cassette tape twice. "Let's talk about that after you listen to the tape."

Sean rubbed the back of his head, fighting off the urge to push the matter.

"We told the sheriff she went to the cemetery, but they couldn't find any trace of her. It was a kayaker who found her, a week later."

"A kayaker?"

Heather pulled a tissue out of the bag and dabbed her eyes. "A quarter mile downriver. She was all tangled up in a fallen tree, half-submerged."

"Holy hell," Sean said, shaking his head. "What happened?"

Heather drew in a long breath. "The sheriff thinks she slipped. But look at this wall." Heather craned her neck to face it. "Unless she was walking on it—which she'd *never* do—she couldn't have just *fallen in.*"

Sean looked over the stone structure. "Totally. That makes no sense."

Heather stood and walked back to the wall. She placed both hands on the top and leaned over, looking down at the river. "When I listened to your cassette tape, it gave me chills. When I heard you describe how Thomas had come from across the river..."

Sean pushed himself up from the bench and skirted around it, sidling beside Heather. She visored her eyes with her hand and gazed across the river, as if focused on something unseen, way off in the distance.

"My mom asked me to go with her that night, but I said no. It's my biggest regret now. If I'd gone, maybe she'd still be around." Heather paused to wipe her eyes. "Anyway, I'm sure of this: My mom did *not* just fall in."

Sean imagined Marilyn here, in the darkness, near this wall. How had she ended up in the river?

"Something bad is going on here, Sean."

When he turned to face Heather, she looked intently into his eyes, a fresh flow of tears streaming down her cheeks.

"I can't bring my mom back, but I also can't let her die for nothing. I need to find out what's happening."

Sean swallowed hard, fighting back his own tears. "Ever since Karl died, I've felt guilty. I'm always thinking about how if I'd done things differently, maybe he'd still be here."

"I know the feeling," she said, wiping her cheeks. "We can't change the past, though."

"No. But knowing that you're doing something about it makes a difference. You've picked up where your mom left off." Sean made a fist and pressed it against his mouth, questioning whether he should get more involved before listening to the tape. He brushed the hesitation aside. "I need to feel like I'm doing something, too. Can I help?"

Heather sniffed. "Most definitely. I reached out to you, hoping you might be willing to. You were my only option, and I didn't even need to ask. So, thank you."

She wiped her cheeks, picked up the satchel, and pivoted to face the cemetery. "I'm leaving you with that tape. After you listen to it and have had a chance to digest it, we'll talk again."

He nodded, and she set off toward her car.

As Heather crossed the roadway, she spun around and gave Sean a parting wave and a gorgeous teary-eyed smile.

Chapter 5

As soon as Sean had the Granada running with the AC cranked, he fished his Walkman out of his floor console, inserted the cassette tape, and positioned the headphones over his ears. He pushed Play and shifted into gear. By the time he turned onto the riverside roadway, a teenager began talking.

There's a lot more to the story than I told the deputies. I'm gonna tell you everything here, though. Some of this would have gotten me into trouble. Other stuff...well, the deputies would've thought I was mental.

There were supposed to be four of us that night, but Justin and Billy backed out. I should've too. The whole thing was wrong from the beginning. Problem is, when Marcus got an idea in his head, there was no stopping him.

It all started with an after-school scouting expedition. That's what Marcus called it. All four of us were there for that, but Marcus wouldn't tell us where we were going. Each time I asked, he'd say, "That's for me to know and you to find out, Jackass." I always hated that my parents named me Jackson. I go by Jack, which is better, but still makes me an easy target. Marcus was the king of name-calling. Even with me, supposedly his best friend.

We all piled into his '72 Olds Delta 88. That car was a total beater. The floorboards were so rusted out, you could lift the carpets and piss onto the road. We called it "visiting the rest stop." Just so you know, *I* never pulled that stunt.

Marcus had installed a kick-ass sound system worth way more than the car, and he mounted these massive speakers into the rear window deck. He was obsessed with Rush. Don't get me wrong, we *all* thought Rush rocked. It's just that Marcus never listened to anything *except* Rush.

On that day, it was their latest album, *Moving Pictures.* I got a kick out of watching Marcus try to air drum to "Tom Sawyer" while he drove. He looked pretty stupid because he couldn't keep up with Neil Peart. Then again, not many could. I mean, Peart's the greatest drummer of all time.

The music was blaring, and one of those speakers was a foot from my head. It was so loud I could barely hear myself think. But by the time we finished the joint we were passing around, I wasn't thinking straight, anyway.

Okay, Marilyn, I see the way you're looking at me. I'll get back to the point now.

Marcus switched off the music when he started driving past the village cemetery. I was *so* hoping he'd drive on by. When he turned in, I asked what we were doing there.

"I told you, Jackass," he said. "Scouting expedition."

My ears were ringing, and I was too high to argue, so I tried to make myself chill.

He pulled the car into the parking area just inside that giant arched gateway at the entrance. Billy, sitting in the front passenger seat, pointed out how Marcus didn't park straight. Even from the back seat, I could see Billy was right.

Marcus stuck his middle finger in Billy's face and asked him if he was the parking patrol.

Further inside the cemetery, two other cars were

parked in the driveways, and we could see some people visiting graves. Climbing out of that car into the cemetery felt so weird. Maybe I was just being paranoid, but it seemed like we were being watched. We had no business being there, so I prayed nobody would ask what we were up to.

It turned out we weren't going far, though. Marcus stopped at a strange little hill about four feet high and fifteen feet across, encircled with white posts holding a chain looped all the way around. He spread open his arms and said, "This is it."

Billy asked, "What is?"

Marcus pointed at the mound. "We're going to dig a bone out of here."

The three of us stared at where he was pointing. Billy eventually asked what I'm sure we were all wondering. "There are bones in there?"

Marcus said, "Damn right. Lots of them. But I only need one."

Nobody spoke for a while. It was Justin who eventually asked, "What for?"

Marcus smacked him on the side of the head and said, "What do you think, dipshit? The most wicked keepsake ever."

Justin asked why Marcus wanted a bone as a keepsake.

Marcus gave his pissed-off look and said, "Why wouldn't I? You can get one too."

Justin told him, "I don't want a goddamned bone."

I kept my mouth shut, although I didn't want one either.

Billy spoke up, though. He said, "Me neither. We're talking bad luck to the max, man."

Marcus blew a big puff of breath out of his lips, then told us, "It's a *good* luck charm, you idiots. These aren't just any bones. They're Indian bones. They have magical powers." He pointed at a stone marker a little way down the circle. I could read it from where we stood. It read: **BURIAL SITE OF INDIAN MARTYRS 1782**

Chills ran down my spine. I asked him what this was.

Marcus turned and walked away, waving over his shoulder for us to follow. He stopped in front of one of those brown Ohio historical marker signs about ten yards off. "A DAY OF SHAME" stood out in the headline. I scanned through the text below, which described something about how a group of Pennsylvania militiamen massacred 96 innocent Indians, including women and children. At *this* site. I spun back around and stared at the grassy little hill.

Just to be clear: this wasn't like those Indian mounds all over Ohio that we learned about in school. Indians built those for ceremonies. They're called earthworks, and they're bigger and much older. No, this was nothing like that. This was a place where massacred people were buried just two hundred years ago.

I felt like my knees were going to give out. There was a tree nearby, so I leaned against its trunk.

Marcus told us to check out the date.

It was March 8, 1782.

Billy asked, "So?"

Marcus pointed out how next week it would be the eighth of March.

Billy shrugged.

"This is 1982," Marcus said. "Monday will be two hundred years later, exactly. That's when we're going digging."

Nobody said anything, but Billy and Justin's faces told me *they* weren't going to be there on the eighth of March.

I tried pulling out too—several times, but Marcus wouldn't have it. He said, "If those bastards are too chicken-shit, that's fine. It's always been you and me anyway, since kindergarten, right?"

It was true. Marcus and I had been in the same kindergarten class. So, maybe I put up with his crap more than others were willing to. I was pissed that Billy and Justin weaseled out, but I couldn't blame them. I convinced myself there was no harm in going along for the ride. Pfft. Little did I know...

Marcus decided we'd go at nine o'clock. It got dark around seven, but too many people would still be out then. He insisted it wouldn't take long, and we'd be home by ten thirty, which was my weeknight curfew. Marcus's parents were divorced, and he lived with his mom. She didn't give a rat's ass what he did. It was a different story for me, with my strict parents.

Marcus drove, and on the way, he smoked a joint all by himself. I'm one of those people who gets revved up and paranoid from smoking pot. The idea of being in that cemetery at night was intense enough. I couldn't imagine doing it high.

He parked his Oldsmobile at one of the churches near the town square. When he popped the trunk, there were two shovels inside.

I backed away and said, "I told you, I ain't digging."

Marcus shrugged. He called me a pussy under his breath, but he put the shovel back in the trunk and closed it. I was shocked he let it go so easily, but either way, I was not about to dig up any bones.

During the two-block hike to the back end of the cemetery, not a single car passed by, and the only person we saw was some guy walking his German shepherd. I'll never forget how that dog growled at Marcus, like it knew he was up to no good. That was it, though. It was a cold night, so I'm sure that helped us go unnoticed.

The street lights ended at the graveyard. We headed into darkness from there. Part of me was glad to leave the spotlight, but most of me was wigging out from walking into a cemetery in the dark.

And when I say it was dark, it was *major* dark. There was only a little sliver of moon that night, so we had to walk slowly to avoid bumping into the headstones. A few of the graves had lit candles sitting on them, inside a votive so the wind wouldn't blow them out. It was totally creepy. At that point, I was glad I hadn't smoked any of that joint, because I don't think my nerves could've handled it.

Halfway there, Marcus whispered, "Nobody's allowed in the cemetery after sunset, so if anyone sees us, run like hell into those woods." He pointed to a patch of trees at the far end of the graveyard.

I gave him the okay sign, and neither of us said anything else until we got there. Marcus was normally a first-class loudmouth, but I think even he was too nervous to talk.

He immediately stepped over the chain circling the burial place, climbed up to the center of the hill, and stabbed his spade into the mound. I stood there and watched for a minute, feeling like I was going to ralph.

The only light was a lantern hanging from a metal pole near the stone marker. Inside the lantern was a lit candle. I suppose the candlelight was a sign of remembrance, but the light was so weak it only made everything look extra spooky.

Thinking about what he was doing was too much, so I crossed the driveway and sat on one of the closest headstones, maybe twenty yards away. Like keeping my distance might sugarcoat my involvement.

I wasn't sitting there long when all of a sudden, Marcus dropped the shovel, hurdled over the chain, and started jetting my way. "Split!" he yelled. "It's a cop!"

I jumped up and followed him as he ran past me into that end of the graveyard toward the patch of woods. When I looked over my shoulder, I spotted a car bookin' toward us with a rack of lights on its roof.

I turned back to face my path just in time to dodge an extra-large headstone I was about to slam into. With it being dark, we couldn't run fast. We'd only made it halfway to the trees when the car turned into the entrance, its headlights sweeping through that graveyard section.

Marcus jumped behind a big headstone and yelled, "Hide!"

I dove behind a different grave marker, one of those tall, narrow, pointed ones—kind of pencil-shaped, but square.

The rational part of my brain knew Marcus had the right idea: don't panic. We would have been seen if we had kept running, even though that's exactly what I *wanted* to do. I forced myself to sit at the base of the headstone, pressing my back tightly against the cold granite. I pulled in my shoulders so no part of me would stick out, and I stretched my legs straight, low to the ground.

I was trying not to move, but this was tough because I was gasping to catch my breath. That's the other thing that freaked me out: I was panting, sending giant puffs of vapor into the air with each breath. I thought for sure the cop would notice that, so I started breathing into my sleeve, which did the trick.

After the sheriff's car rolled to a stop, a bright beam of light swept across the graveyard. I knew exactly what it was: one of those spotlights they had mounted on the door.

Speaking in a forceful whisper, Marcus told me not to move. I totally wanted to jump up and bolt. Instead, I gritted my teeth and tried to hold my breath. It was a warped feeling, knowing if this didn't work, I was basically giving myself up.

The light passed over us several times. Then it went out. My heart was pounding so hard I could hear it in my eardrums, but after a while, I could make out the sound of the car driving off.

Marcus crawled out from the shadows and yelled, "Hell, yeah! I *knew* that would work!"

I told him to shut up while I climbed to my feet and brushed myself off. Then I warned him, "I still say we're going to get busted."

He didn't buy it, though. He said, "The coast is clear now, man. Time to get my magical bone."

If only I had driven, I'd have left Marcus there by himself. Instead, I went back to the same headstone and sat again while Marcus jogged over to the mound.

I mostly kept my eyes on the roadway, but occasionally scanned the rest of the perimeter. It was on one of these scans when I saw him. I froze and did a double-take. I leaned forward and squinted, expecting to convince myself it was just a harmless shadow. But it wasn't. Someone was sitting on the stone wall near the river. I just about pissed myself.

I called to Marcus, careful to keep my voice low.

He didn't hear me between the noise of his digging and his concentration.

I watched, waiting for the figure to move. A thought crossed my mind: maybe this was just another teenager.

I pushed myself up and crossed the drive, moving casually. No need to make a scene. As I got close to the burial place, I called out to Marcus again.

This time, he stopped.

"Someone's here," I said. But when I turned back in the direction of the river, the figure was gone.

I pointed to where the silhouette had been and told him, "They were right there!"

"You're mental," Marcus said, and he went back to digging.

I checked over the full length of the wall, but there was no sign of anyone. It was insane. How could a person just vanish? I was spazzing out by this point, so I begged Marcus, "Let's hightail it, man."

He stepped into the hole he'd been digging. It was knee deep now. He said, "I'm almost there. It can't be much further."

There was a maintenance shack nearby, blocking part of my view. I headed over to it and ducked into its shadows. I circled the building, and when I rounded the front corner, that was when I got clobbered.

This part didn't come back to me until later. With time, I pieced together a faint memory of something solid slamming into the side of my head and pain exploding in my skull.

The next thing I remember is hearing this horrible scraping sound. I tried opening my eyes, but my head and neck ached something fierce. At the time, it seemed like that awful noise was causing the pain, but after a while, I figured out they were two separate things.

Eventually, I managed to open my eyes, but then I realized I was lying face down, with my nose pressed into the ground. I rolled over and brushed the grass and dirt off.

Something sticky was on my neck, and I followed it up to the side of my head. It was blood. I had a bump the size of a baseball up there, and a major gash where the blood was oozing out from.

The scraping noise was still there, but it was getting quieter. I fought through the pain and pushed myself onto my knees, turning to get a read on the sound.

I blinked, trying to make sense of what I was seeing. It looked like a boy in his early teens, heading down the drive toward the river, dragging a shovel. The head of that spade scraping on the asphalt was causing that maddening sound.

It was so dark that all I could see were shadows, so I couldn't describe him, other than he was sickly skinny. Then, another thing hit me: he wasn't wearing enough clothes for how cold it was. Like, no jacket even. Just a ragged shirt and pants. And his shoes...they weren't real shoes. They looked like a grody pair of my dad's slippers or something.

He crossed the roadway, and the shovel went silent as he dragged it over a patch of grass. When he got to the wall, he picked it up and tossed it over. Then, he climbed up the wall, and that's when my vision went blurry. I squeezed my eyes shut for a few seconds, and that helped. But when I looked back, he was gone. Just like that, he'd disappeared.

My head hurt so bad I could barely think, so it took a while before it hit me: Was that Marcus's shovel? I had forgotten all about Marcus.

The maintenance shack was blocking my view of him and the burial site. After climbing to my feet, I leaned against the wall to steady myself.

It felt like a mega freight train was passing through my head, but when I touched the bump, some of the blood had hardened. I figured that meant the worst of the bleeding had stopped.

With one hand sliding against the shack to help me stay upright, I circled it and peeked around the back corner. I saw the mound, but at first, Marcus was nowhere in sight.

Then I saw something crumpled over the chain, on the opposite side. It looked like a pile of garbage, but...

I already knew it wasn't that.

I called out for Marcus, loud enough for him to hear, but not so loud that I could be heard by anyone else.

The lump didn't move.

I staggered toward it, feeling like I'd lost my sense of balance, trying to focus my eyes while pain thudded in my head.

I went around the mound, not trusting myself to step over the chain without tripping. As I rounded it, I noticed something weird: there was no hole in the middle. Did Marcus fill it all back in? If so, he even went as far as to piece back the top layer of sod.

When I reached him, I dropped to my knees and said his name.

He didn't respond and never moved.

The way he looked, I was afraid to touch him. He was slumped over the chain at his stomach, his legs inside the circle, his upper body on the outside, with his face pretty much planted in the grass.

My head was majorly foggy, but I started feeling panicky through the haze.

I looked down the driveway and scanned across the stone wall, half expecting to see that figure again. But I saw nothing.

I crawled forward and shook Marcus's shoulders, saying, "C'mon, man!"

When he still didn't react, I grabbed him around the waist and hoisted his legs over the chain. He was all dead weight, and the strain of it had me seeing stars.

I rested a minute to recover, questioning whether I should just go for help. But how could I do that without getting us into trouble?

After crawling back over to his head, I put my hand on it and felt the same stickiness I had felt on my own. I groaned as my throat tightened. I felt like I was about to scream, cry, or pass out...or all of the above. I fought it off, though, and pulled Marcus toward me, rolling his head onto my lap. Something gross flopped over onto my thigh, and I yelped.

If I'd had any light, I would've recognized it, but that candle lantern across the mound was useless from our spot. In my confused state, I thought it was a mutilated squirrel.

But when I tried brushing it away, I couldn't. It was attached to the back of his head. I ran my fingers over it to feel what it was and realized it wasn't fur.

It was hair...Marcus's hair.

Except it was all bound together in a sticky clump, not on his head. A long strip, the bottom end still attached to the back of his head. I put my other hand on the top of his head, and that's when I screamed.

Marcus had been scalped.

Chapter 6

Sean Davidson drove fast, swearing all the way, hoping to make up some of the fifteen minutes he'd lost from flooding the Granada when he first tried starting it.

When the cemetery came into view, he pressed the Stop button on his Walkman, and the title track to Pink Floyd's latest album, *The Final Cut,* ended abruptly. Heather Warner's white Chevette appeared as he rounded the bend, parked in the same spot as that hot July day, over a month prior.

Sean wiped his palms dry on his pant legs, adjusted the rearview mirror, and fussed with his hair before turning into the entrance drive.

While parking the Granada beside the Chevette, he spotted Heather ten yards away, reading a historical marker sign. She turned around and gave a hello nod. His nerves reacted, and he accidentally squeezed the wheel, beeping the horn. *Dumbass*, he called himself, then gave her a wave—the cool variety, the raised-hand type.

He spit the piece of Nicorette gum he'd been chewing into its used wrapper and killed the engine. The unseasonable late-summer chill hit him as he stepped out, like a first taste of the coming fall. "Sorry I'm late." He circled the car door and swung it closed.

"I just got here a few minutes ago," Heather said, walking toward him. This time, she wore jeans and a colorful, baggy sweater.

Sean stopped cold when he recognized the burial site Jack had described in the recording, just off to the side. About fifteen feet across and four feet high at its center, the mound was covered in grass and encircled with white posts, holding a chain that looped around the perimeter.

"How come I didn't notice this last time? It's not far from where I parked."

Heather locked her gaze on it. "It's one of those things that doesn't stand out until you know what it is. Once you do, you can't *not* see it."

They veered around the circle to the spot where a long iron pipe had been inserted into the ground. The candle lantern Jack had described hung from it. Beneath it, a stone epitaph was embedded in the ground. Sean read the carved letters:

BURIAL SITE OF INDIAN MARTYRS 1782

The scene left him breathless. Wanting desperately to make sense of it, he asked, "Do they know why this happened?"

Heather pointed over her shoulder with her thumb. "That sign talks about it. During the Revolutionary War, a group of militiamen rounded up 96 peaceful Indians, mostly women and children. They were accused of being spies and executed."

Sean swallowed, trying to imagine it. Almost one hundred peaceful people, mostly women and children. Everything about it was hard to stomach.

"So senseless." Heather shook her head. "A war crime."

"An atrocity." Sean's words came out in a croak. Unable to read the historical marker from where he stood, he stared at it anyway, blinking away the sting in his eyes.

"They were innocent..." Heather paused and sniffed. "...but they refused to fight their accusers. They prayed and sang hymns instead. They had joined a Moravian Christian mission here."

"Moravian." Sean repeated the word, turning it over.

"Yes. That's where this village got its name."

"And they're all buried here?" Sean swept his hand across the little hill in front of them.

Heather frowned and nodded. "They threw the dead bodies in the mission house and burned it down. Afterward, the missionaries gathered the bones and buried them here. See that log cabin behind us?"

Sean turned and looked at where she pointed. The log structure stood forty yards away, beyond a clearing, at the cemetery's edge.

"It's a replica of the mission house," Heather explained. "It's built on the original foundation."

Sean tried to picture the horrific act that had taken place there, conjuring an image of the log mission house burning.

"See that stone monument?"

With the interruption of Heather's words, the massacre scene fell away, and the surrounding cemetery snapped back into focus. Sean turned his eyes to where Heather was pointing. A massive obelisk rose from the ground, not far from the front entrance of the mission house.

"They put that there on the one-hundredth anniversary of the massacre," she said. "In honor of the victims."

Twice the height of the mission house, the monument reached skyward in the gap between the surrounding trees. Sean panned across the graveyard that surrounded this clearing. The obelisk stood far taller than anything else in the cemetery, emphasizing the magnitude of the tragedy.

"I don't remember learning about this in school," he said.

"Me neither," Heather said. "I don't know why."

They stood silently for a long stretch before she asked, "So, what did you think of Jack's recording?"

Sean drew in a long breath. "It blew my mind. I listened to it half a dozen times."

Heather gave a humorless laugh. "I've got you topped."

"I remember hearing the kids at school talking about how someone had been murdered in Moravian Village."

Heather furrowed her brow and considered this. "That would have been almost two and a half years ago now."

"Yeah, that sounds right. It's a different school district, and Clarkton is far enough away that I didn't pay much attention. I'd pretty much forgotten all about it. I never even made the connection that it happened right near Grand-Bob's house."

"Do you believe Jack's story?"

"For sure. But if I hadn't lived through the thing with Karl, I probably wouldn't have."

"See, that's the thing." Heather chewed her lower lip. "None of us have shared our stories—"

"Because no one would believe us."

"Yeah, you pegged it." Heather took a deep breath. "So, was it Thomas who Jack saw?"

Sean exhaled audibly. "Sure sounds like it. Don't you think?"

A cool breeze blew. Heather turned into the wind and adjusted the scrunchy in her hair. "I do. And so did my mom."

Suddenly, Sean felt glad he'd reached out to Marilyn Warner. But then again, by getting her involved...

He pushed aside the thought and rotated back to face the burial site. "Did Jack get in trouble for digging here?"

"According to my mom's notes, the sheriff never found out. Remember how Jack said the hole had been filled back in?"

Sean nodded.

"My mom suspected Thomas did that after scalping Marcus."

"So, what exactly did Jack tell the investigators?"

"Just that they'd been attacked. Two innocent teenagers walking through the cemetery on a nighttime dare."

"And the sheriff bought it?"

"Apparently. Since the mound had been put back in order, I guess the investigators were none the wiser about what they'd *really* been up to."

"Have you spoken with Jack?"

Heather turned and started walking toward the driveway. She motioned for Sean to follow and led him across it, into the newest section of the graveyard.

A few rows in, she stopped in front of a simple headstone. Sean stepped beside her and read the inscription:

Marcus Tridick
October 13, 1965 — March 8, 1982

So, here he was. How ironic: the asshole had been buried within eyeshot of the spot where karma had gotten the best of him.

"He didn't die from being scalped," Heather said, startling Sean. "Scalpings aren't always fatal, anyway. The autopsy report concluded he died from a blow to the head."

Sean stared at the headstone and slowly wrung his hands.

Heather beckoned him forward. Twenty feet away, she stopped again, pointing with her chin at another marker, this one sitting atop a band of recently disturbed ground:

Jackson "Jack" McCarthy
December 2, 1965 — March 25, 1984

Sean stopped in his tracks as a knot twisted in his gut. *Jack's dead too?* The question formed in Sean's head, but the words died in his mouth.

Heather flashed him a confirming glance. "Jack OD'd shortly after my mom died."

"OD'd, as in..."

She bowed her head, turned, and started walking toward the river. "Heroin overdose," Heather said over her shoulder.

"Shit..." Sean grappled with this as he stared at the headstone. A moment later, he pulled away, hurrying to catch up to Heather.

"Let that be a warning," she said as he drew in.

"Pfft. You don't need to warn me about heroin." Sean felt Heather looking at him, but he fixed his gaze on the riverside wall they were heading toward. "The summer after tenth grade, I did landscaping. I worked with an old ex-con biker dude. He warned me never to touch heroin. He was talking from experience. So, even back when I was messing around with drugs, I knew to stay away from heroin."

"You don't do drugs anymore?"

"Nope. I quit that stuff after Karl died. Cold turkey. Even drinking. I couldn't get it out of my head how if we hadn't been out there getting stoned, he'd still be here."

"Good for you." Heather gave him the cutest smile.

Sean felt his face getting hot. Fortunately, a car was heading their way, saving him with an outside distraction. They stepped aside and waited for the vehicle to pass.

As they crossed the road, Heather asked, "Did you notice the date?"

He cocked his head and looked at her. "What date?"

"The date of the massacre."

"1782."

"Right, but the actual day?"

Sean shrugged as they arrived at the stone wall. "Help me out."

"The eighth of March. Isn't that the same date you had your run-in with Thomas?"

Sean's heart stopped. "Now that you mention it, yes. It was March 8, 1983."

Heather stared out over the river. "So, that was exactly one year after Marcus was killed."

He rocked back on his heels. "Wow. That's weird."

She turned to face him. "It was my mom who had made that connection."

He scratched the back of his neck. Was this just a strange coincidence?

"And guess what date my mother drowned?"

Sean stiffened. He narrowed his eyes and studied her. "No way."

"Yes, way." Heather massaged her temple with two fingertips. "The eighth of March, this year. 1984."

He leaned out over the wall and blew out a long breath.

"She made a point of coming here exactly one year after your encounter with Thomas. Two years after Marcus was scalped."

Sean buried his face in his hands as he tried to absorb this. "So, what you're saying..."

Heather cleared her throat and placed her palm over her mouth, mustering what she'd say next. "My mom...I'm sure of it...she *didn't* just fall in."

Sean glared down the length of the stonework, imagining what Jack had described: a figure sitting on the wall, watching from the nighttime shadows.

One year later, the same presence—Thomas, as he'd called himself—had somehow crossed the flooded river, intruding on his and Karl's fireside party.

Then, again, one year later to the day, Marilyn, somewhere near this very spot...what had she seen before ending up in the river?

"Stop that."

Sean's dark musings dissolved with Heather's command. He turned to face her.

She smiled. "You'll get arthritis."

He realized he'd been cracking his knuckles. He chuckled. "My mom's been telling me that since I started when I was nine. Do you think it's true?"

Heather shrugged. "That's what they always say."

"I'm in serious trouble, then. Nowadays, I don't even notice when I'm doing it. I can't seem to break the habit."

"Try wearing mittens."

Before Sean could formulate a clever comeback, Heather moved on. “Hey, is there any place to eat around here?”

Instead of working out an answer to her question, Sean wondered whether this might be an opening for him. Before long, he realized he didn’t have an answer to either question, so he focused on what she had asked. “There’s no fast food anywhere around. Maybe one of the shops on the square serves lunch.” He almost let it go there, but inspiration sparked in his brain. “I can take you. I’m starving.” He wasn’t, really.

Heather didn’t respond immediately, which made Sean think she was preparing to reject his suggestion.

“Okay. But let’s take both cars so I can hit the road from there.”

Unable to hold back a grin, Sean set off for his car and waved for Heather to follow.

Chapter 7

Sean pulled into the first of two adjoining open street parking spaces at the town's main intersection. As Heather maneuvered her white Chevette behind him, he popped a fresh piece of Nicorette gum into his mouth and climbed out.

"Sorry if you were gagging," he said when she opened her car door. "My car burns oil. The engine needs new rings."

As she stepped into the street, she asked, "Is that expensive?"

"Yeah, like five hundred bucks. It's not worth sinking that into this junker. Anyway, I won't be driving it much during the school year. OSU doesn't let freshmen keep a car on campus."

Heather led the way between the cars to the sidewalk. "So, you're going to Ohio State?"

"I leave next week."

"Cool. I'm thinking of going there too," Heather said.

He gave a little laugh. "It's a popular choice. Of all the students in my class going to college, half are heading there."

Sean held up at the curb and scanned the single block of storefronts. Straight across the street, a shop bearing a sign reading "Moravi-Yum Donuts" stood out. A hand-painted placard hung in its window, declaring, "WE MAKE SANDWICHES TOO!" Sean pointed that way. "That might be our only option."

Heather licked her lips. "A sandwich and a doughnut. Sounds stellar!"

He led the way across the street, not bothering with the crosswalk. "What grade are you in?"

"Starting twelfth."

"So, you'll be making college applications soon."

Heather nodded. "I'm thinking about Kent State, too. My boyfriend is about to start there. He wants me to join him."

Sean felt the letdown of this revelation, but he tried to hide his reaction. Although this was her first mention of a boyfriend, Sean figured he should not be surprised. Babes like her have guys coming on to them all the time—guys who know how to make their moves, unlike him.

"Hey, can I bum a piece of gum?" she asked.

Sean chuckled, glad she had interrupted his insecurity wallow. "Only if you like gum that tastes like pepper."

Heather scrunched her nose as she skipped onto the curb. "Pepper gum?"

"It's Nicorette. It tastes peppery. Kind of makes your mouth tingle, too."

"You're trying to quit smoking?"

"Yeah. I'm one week in. I took what was left in the box from when my mom quit smoking." Sean raised a finger to his lips in the *shhh* gesture. "Hoping she won't check that box anytime soon."

"Well, good for you!" Heather bobbed her head in approval as they turned toward the doughnut shop. "For quitting, not the thievery."

"I'm probably addicted to this stuff now."

"It's better than smoking. So, what will you be studying?"

"Biology." Sean hustled ahead to open the door.

"Hmmm...a gentleman." Heather thanked him with a pretty smile as she led the way inside.

Sean felt himself blushing. He told himself to say something clever, but before long, too much time had passed. He pretended to study the menu board, hoping Heather would shift her attention there, too.

A man emerged from the back, wiping his hands on his apron. Sean did a double-take. The guy looked just like the Big Boy restaurant mascot. Same round face and Elvis-style hairdo. He even wore overalls underneath the apron. The overalls were white, though. He must've known the red checker pattern would have been too much.

They each gave Big Boy their order, and he went to work on their sandwiches while they settled into one of the bistro tables beside the shop's window.

"So, biology, huh?" Heather tilted her head at him from across the table. "What made you pick that?"

Sean lost track of the question for a spell, tripped up by Heather's stunning amber eyes. Suddenly self-conscious that she might notice him leering at her like a weirdo, he turned to the window and faked watching a truck drive by. A distant inner voice reminded him that he owed her a response. He shrugged. "Eeny meeny miny moe."

Heather laughed.

"I feel lame because I don't know what to study," Sean explained, turning back to face her, but trying to resist the draw of her eyes. "All I know is I don't want to study accounting. My dad's an accountant, so guess what my parents want me to be?"

"Hmmm..." Heather pressed a finger to her lips, feigning deep thought.

He grinned. "What about you?"

She shrugged in turn. “Pretty much the same here. I’m dabbling in writing. So, maybe English.” Her eyes skirted away from his, and she turned to face the window as she fussed with the gold locket hanging from her neck. “My mom studied English.”

Sean wanted to say something comforting, but couldn’t find the words. He stared at the paper napkin in front of him, with his car keys resting in the center of it.

After a while, Heather let out an almost imperceptible sigh, then popped open her can of 7 Up and took a sip.

Sean followed her cue and opened his root beer. “I associate biology with Karl. We took it together. I think he was the only one in the class who wanted to dissect that frog.”

Heather shivered at her own memory of the dreaded high school science rite of passage. “That was horrible!” She flicked at her pop can’s Sta-Tab, making a *boing-boing-boing* sound. “Do you think Karl would’ve studied biology?”

Sean chewed the inside of his cheek as he considered this. “Could be. It’s funny, though. We never talked about college. I guess we were just focused on the present.”

Big Boy brought over a tray with their sandwiches.

They lapsed into silence as they ate until Sean spoke up. “So, Marcus was killed in 1982…”

Heather swallowed a bite and wiped her mouth with a napkin. “Right.”

“On the same date, but in 1983, Karl and I ran into Thomas.”

“Correct.”

“Then, also on the same date, but this year, 1984, your mother drowned.”

She nodded.

“Who died before Marcus?”

Heather put down her sandwich. “Nobody.”

“Nobody?”

She shook her head. “Not as far as my mom could find. I read through her notebook. She had dug through old newspapers. Going back fifty years, she couldn’t find a single case of suspicious deaths on that day in Moravian Village.”

“So, what started it, then?”

“Yeah, that’s the question, isn’t it?” Heather tucked her hair behind her ears. “My mom had two theories. Maybe it started on the 200th anniversary of the massacre. Or maybe Marcus digging in the burial mound caused it.”

Sean leaned back in his chair. “Like something got awakened.”

“Bingo. And that triggered the start of a new...curse. I don’t know, is that what you’d call it?”

Sean ignored the question, figuring she wasn’t expecting a response. “Have you thought about—”

“What’s going to happen next March?”

He nodded.

Heather leaned forward and balled her hands into fists. “I can’t *stop* thinking about it. I’d be a dip if I thought this would just magically end.”

“For sure. That thing’s still out there.”

“But here’s the problem: My mom was the only one who knew what was happening. Now she’s gone, and no one else has a clue other than you and me.”

Sean chewed his lower lip. “What about your father?”

Heather shook her head. “My dad’s been struggling since my mom died. I tried talking to him about the possibility that she was killed just once. He got *so* upset.”

Both of them fell into silent thought. Eventually, Sean spoke. "So, if we just pretended none of this was happening..."

After he trailed off without finishing the question, Heather completed the thought. "How many more innocent people would die?"

Sean narrowed his eyes. "One person's been killed each year—"

Heather raised a finger to interrupt. "It could've been more. You could've been a goner too if you'd taken a drink like Karl did."

Sean pressed his fist against his mouth. "And Thomas had probably left Jack for dead."

Heather leaned forward with her hands clenched on the table's edge. "I used to think the goal was to figure out what's happening. To solve the mystery. But now, I know that's not enough." She locked eyes with Sean. "This thing must be stopped."

Sean started to respond, but hesitated. He rubbed his chin. "Most definitely. But for me, it's not just that." He paused again, trying to find the right words. "I can't bring Karl back, but I can at least get some vengeance."

Heather's eyes took on a sheen. She blinked repeatedly. "I feel the same way about my mom."

"Karl would do that for me."

"And so would my mother." Heather sniffed and dabbed the corners of her eyes with the napkin. "So, we're not just trying to figure out what's going on here—"

Sean Davidson held up his hands, cutting her off. "No, that's not enough." He clenched his jaw and sucked in a breath through his teeth. "We need to get this sonofabitch."

Chapter 8

When he arrived at the Moravian Village town center, Sean found wide-open street parking. It was late morning on a weekday, but not yet close enough to Christmas that people were off work. Most of the schools had let out, though, including Sean's. Heather Warner's too, although her white Chevette was nowhere in sight. As planned, he arrived ten minutes early.

He parked the Granada in front of Moravi-Yum Donuts and stepped out, pulling his jacket closed against the cold. A few flurries fell, but the weather forecast wasn't calling for accumulating snow. With less than a week to go, it wasn't looking like Homer County would be having a white Christmas.

The jingle of the bells hanging over the door summoned the Big Boy restaurant mascot look-alike man, who met Sean at the counter. After ordering two apple fritters and two coffees, Sean stood beside the bistro tables, watching for the Chevette.

Within minutes, he spotted the car. He wiped his palms dry on the thigh of his jeans before gathering the doughnut box and cardboard coffee caddy.

Heather pulled up behind the Granada and waved as he walked out into the cold.

What a babe, he thought. He had tried not to look forward to seeing her so much, but the four months since he'd seen her had seemed much longer. With his hands full, he responded with a smiling head nod as he squeezed between the cars.

"Watcha got there?" she asked as she stepped out, holding a pair of mittens and a knitted hat.

"Brunch. I hope you like coffee and apple fritters."

"That's so sweet! I mean that literally *and* figuratively." Heather grinned. "I like coffee, but never tasted an apple fritter."

"You don't know what you've been missing. They're my fave."

It would have been an awkward hug anyway, but being unprepared for it and having his hands full, Sean reacted clumsily when he found himself in Heather's embrace. He leaned in, basically letting *her* hug *him*, keeping his focus on holding the coffee steady to avoid pouring it on her. Sean had grown up in a non-hugging family, so he wasn't exactly comfortable with what seemed to be an increasingly common practice.

"Want cream or sugar?" Sean asked in the middle of it, then realized how ungraceful his timing was.

She released him and smiled. "I drink it black. Who's driving?"

"I will," Sean said, placing the apple fritters on the roof so he could open the door. "You just drove ninety minutes, so you get a break. Plus, I patched my muffler, so it's not so loud anymore. Hop in."

Heather arranged the coffees in the floor console and then peeked into the doughnut box. "Mmmm," she said approvingly, picking one fritter out. She took a bite. "Mmmm," she repeated, this time with more emphasis. "Or as we used to say when we were kids, scrumptious!"

"Told you so." Sean started the car, checked for oncoming vehicles, and then took a U-turn across the empty street.

Heather wiped the fritter glaze from her lips. "Will Grand-Bob be there?"

He nodded. "This will be the first time I've seen him since Karl's funeral."

"Are you nervous?"

Sean considered this, bobbing his head back and forth as he turned onto the state highway. "I don't know if that's the right word. It'll be weird, though."

They crossed the bridge over the river, where the surroundings abruptly transitioned from small-town residential into rural countryside.

"But he was okay with you coming?"

Sean took a swig of coffee. "He seemed to be. But I also think he was shocked to hear from me."

"Can't blame him. Your calling would've dredged everything back up."

Sean took the first turn after the bridge, a gravel township road surrounded by farm fields. A single farmhouse occupied one side of the road. A little further down stood Grand-Bob's dingy white double-wide mobile home, just before the road reached a dead end. He swallowed at the sight of it.

"You alright?" Heather asked, apparently sensing his discomfort.

"I'm okay." Sean turned into Grand-Bob's gravel drive and followed it to the end, parking in front of the detached garage. He turned off the ignition, swung down the sun visor, and caught the two ticket stubs he'd tucked above it.

Heather wrapped her half-eaten apple fritter in a napkin and placed it in the box beside Sean's untouched one. She pulled out a stick of Lip Smackers lip gloss—7 Up flavored—and wiped some on, then put on her hat and mittens and turned to him. "Ready?"

He tilted his head back, drained his coffee, and swung open his door. "As ready as I'm going to be."

Dressed in a bathrobe, Grand-Bob opened the door even before Sean could ring the doorbell. "Howdy, Buttercup!" He smiled, showing several gaps in his teeth, and stuck out his hand.

"Hi, Grand-Bob," Sean said, shaking. He'd always been a bit uncomfortable calling the man by this family nickname, but it somehow felt more natural now that Karl wasn't here to use it.

"What's your girlfriend's name?"

Sean stammered, "Uh...uh..."

The corners of Heather's mouth turned upward. "I'm Heather. Nice to meet you, Mr. Wolf."

"Pleased to meet you, Heather." Grand-Bob tightened his bathrobe against the cold. "Do you kids want to come in?"

"Thanks, but we can't stay long." Sean made a show of checking his watch. "Heather needs to get back home, so if it's okay, we'll just head around back." Sean pointed with his chin to the corner of the house.

Grand-Bob let out a melancholy sigh, nodded, and took a small step backward, retreating to the warmth of his home. "Do your thing, Sean. Remember, if you ever want to go back there, go right ahead. You don't even need to ask. I don't own the farm field, but the farmer and I are old pals. He won't mind."

"Thanks, Grand-Bob." Sean turned back to the walkway. "I'll probably take you up on that sometime."

Grand-Bob raised a hand as a wave, stepped back into the house, and closed the door.

It had been over a year and a half since that fateful night at the campfire, but Sean's knees instantly weakened when he looked across the field at the strip of riverside trees.

The snow flurries swirled in the wind, magnifying his feeling of disorientation. In the distance, the barren tree branches twitched, caught in the breeze, like skeletal fingers beckoning Sean to return.

As he stared across the field, an ache formed in his chest, like he'd taken a punch. Although Sean had known how tough it would be to visit this location, he'd underestimated the weight of the emotion.

Pulling in a deep breath, he filled his lungs with cold air, which gave him a welcome, numbing sensation. He balled his hands into fists, pushed them into his coat pockets, and stepped into the field.

The half-frozen ground crunched gently underfoot. Sean's heart rate ratcheted up as they proceeded over the corn stubble end rows until his pulse was beating in his eardrums. He told himself to calm down, but he knew it was hopeless.

"How did your first quarter go?" Heather asked.

Her earnest expression told Sean she knew how difficult this was for him. Grateful for the distraction she was trying to serve, his tension released a notch.

"I think okay, but I don't have my grades yet, so we'll see. It was a rude awakening, to be honest. I sailed through high school and hardly ever studied. Can't coast like that in college, though."

"I've heard others say that, too."

Sean figured she was referring to her boyfriend, but he tried not to dwell on it. "It's ironic: I finally became the serious student my parents always wanted me to be, but only after they were no longer there to hound me."

"We do what it takes."

"So, have you picked your school yet?"

"It's between Kent State and Ohio State. I'm applying to both."

Before Sean could figure out how to respond, Heather changed the subject. "What was your best class?"

He chuckled. "They were all a grind, except Music Appreciation."

"Yeah, that sounds awesome."

"I won't have any fun classes this coming quarter. I decided winter quarters will be strictly business. But in the spring, I'm taking scuba diving."

Heather gave him a questioning look. "Where do you learn that?"

"In the swimming pool. Toward the end, we'll do some dives at an old stone quarry off campus."

"Huh. Does this have anything to do with biology?"

"Indirectly. If I get certified, I might be able to land a biology internship next summer. They do environmental surveys in rivers and lakes before approving construction permits. The divers look for endangered mollusks."

"That'd be cool."

"You can say that again." Sean shuddered. "Speaking of cool, it's freezing out here!"

"I'm pretty comfy." Heather raised her eyebrows and pointed both of her mittens at her hat.

"I'm tough," Sean said, flexing his arms. The truth was, he felt foolish for not having brought a hat. He had no intention of admitting it, but he had left it behind simply because he didn't want to give himself hat hair. *Why worry about that? She already has a boyfriend.*

"What's with all those birds?" Heather narrowed her eyes at the hundreds of large, black birds chattering and cawing from the bare branches of the riverside band of trees.

"It's a murder of crows," Sean said.

"A *murder*?"

He shrugged. "For some reason, they call a flock of crows a murder."

"It fits. They're so creepy. Why do they all gather like that?"

"Strength in numbers against predators." The birds suddenly took flight, exploding into the sky in a noisy racket.

As they flew off, Sean looked over his shoulder and gauged that they were past halfway across the field already. Heather's diversion tactic had helped immensely. But as they drew closer to the river, his pulse quickened again. Now, he had no choice but to face the demons of his memory. Even Heather seemed to understand this because she dropped the idle talk for the balance of the trek.

Before long, Sean felt out of breath, partly because of the exertion, but mostly from his rising angst. Gasping, he pointed ahead to the edge of the tree band, just beyond the end row of corn stubble. "The fire pit was just up there."

"Do you think we can still find it?"

Indeed, that was the question. The dusting of snow had collected in pockets, obscuring the ground. Sean slowed his pace, scanning the surface in search of charred remnants. When he noticed a blackened patch, a lump formed in his throat. He veered toward the spot and hovered over it, holding one hand against his cheek.

Heather stepped up beside him. "I know this isn't easy."

Sean could only nod. He tightened his jaw and told himself not to cry as he conjured the scene of that night. Partying here with his best friend until a monster invaded, taking Karl away forever. Anger erupted in Sean's mind.

He took a deep breath, peeled his attention away, and looked toward the river. "Let's get on with it," he said, heading that way.

Heather followed silently.

Sean drew in on a mature tree rooted on the embankment's edge. He stripped a couple of loose pieces of bark away, exposing a solid surface, then fished a piece of cardboard and the two ticket stubs out of his inner jacket pocket. With his fingers frigid, he struggled to remove the two thumbtacks embedded in the cardboard, but eventually managed to extract them. He used them to fasten the tickets to the tree, with a tack securing either end. He stepped back, pushed his hands back into his pockets, and gazed with bleary eyes at the ticket stubs.

"AC/DC?" Heather asked.

"Yeah." Sean sniffed. "That was our first concert. November 1981, at the Richfield Coliseum in Cleveland. We went with my cousins. Karl *loved* AC/DC."

"You had both of the stubs?"

He nodded. "After he died, Mrs. Wolf gave me Karl's record collection. I found his concert stub inside his copy of *For Those About to Rock.* That was the tour we saw."

He stared at the tickets and cleared his throat. "It's a pretty lame memorial, though, isn't it?"

Heather shook her head. "Not at all, Sean. It's beautiful."

Sean wasn't sure what she meant by that, but he let it go. "Did you hear Grand-Bob invite me back anytime?"

"I certainly did. He said you don't even need to ask."

"That's sure convenient for the night of March 8."

Heather rubbed her mittened hand over her mouth. "But won't he think it's weird that you're having a campfire alone?"

Sean let out a long breath as he considered this. "If I tell him I'm having an honorary campfire for Karl on the anniversary of our last campfire, why would he question it?"

Heather kept rubbing her mouth, furrowing her brow. "I see your point." She turned to face Sean. "So, you really think you can lure back Thomas this way?"

"Well, the last time I was here for a campfire on that date, he showed up."

Heather bobbed her head from side to side like she could follow the logic. She turned back to the river, then shifted along the bank, seeking a gap in the trees. She halted and pointed at the stone wall on the other side. "That evergreen shrub growing near the wall would make a good hiding place."

Sean stepped beside her and looked at where she was pointing. "I'd say so. That'll be your secret lookout spot. You watch for him, and warn me when he's coming my way."

"Your walkie-talkies will reach this far?"

"For sure. It's a straight shot across the river, and we won't be far apart."

"So, what time should we take our positions?"

Sean chewed his lip. "I'll need to get the fire started before it gets dark. That'll be around seven. But I'm sure it was after nine when Thomas came to the campfire."

"According to what Jack said, Thomas attacked him and Marcus after nine."

"Sounds like we'll be twiddling our thumbs for a while."

"We're going to get cold being out that long." Heather broke out in a mischievous smile. "You'd better wear a hat."

Sean grinned, but her comment got him thinking about the weather. He looked up at the sky. "I sure hope it's not raining that night. Snow would suck too, but rain would screw up everything."

Heather turned back to face the location of the campfire. "So, you still haven't told me your plan once you've lured him here."

Sean considered this momentarily, then drew an imaginary zipper across his lips. "My lips are sealed, but trust me, it's going to be good."

Chapter 9

SEAN HAD TAKEN THE Granada to Ohio State after winter break and put it in an off-campus storage lot, specifically so he could drive home on the eighth of March.

Luckily, the date fell on a Friday, when his winter quarter schedule carried only two classes, both in the morning. So, when the day Sean thought would never come finally did, he was on the highway heading north from Columbus shortly after one o'clock.

He hadn't told his parents he was coming home, taking advantage of them being at work. Wasting no time upon his three o'clock arrival in Clarkton, he cleaned and vacuumed his car to make it look halfway decent. He even hung one of those pine tree-shaped air fresheners from the rearview mirror to mask the mildewy odor. The activity helped distract him from the simmering dread of what lay ahead after sunset.

Next, Sean loaded up his trunk with the evening's provisions before heading to the hardware store for the supplies he didn't already have on hand.

It was shortly after 5:30 when he parked in front of Moravi-Yum Donuts, half an hour before he was supposed to meet Heather. He reached for the door and noticed the shop's hours were 7:00 a.m.

to 6:00 p.m. *Good thing you're early,* he said to himself. *Get the sandwiches before they close.*

Big Boy came out from the back when the bell above the door jingled. Sean ordered two sandwiches and two drinks. Ten minutes before closing time, he walked out with the food, wondering if he should be forcing himself to eat in his nervous state.

The white Chevette appeared in his rearview mirror just as Sean was getting situated in the Granada. He checked his hair one last time, then stepped out and waved.

Heather waved back and parked in the open space behind him. When she climbed out, Sean said, "It turns out we'll be eating in my car. The shop closes at six."

Heather looked at the shop's hours sign, then her watch. "I'd better hurry up and place my order."

"I've already got it." Sean pointed with his thumb inside his car.

Heather changed course and headed his way, greeting him with a hug. Although he was expecting it this time, Sean didn't quite know what to do with his hands, so his embrace turned out to be less enthusiastic than he meant for it to be. Her lotion or perfume sure smelled good, though.

As she pulled away and headed to the passenger side, Heather said, "It felt *so weird* coming back to this town. This thing's been eating me alive."

Sean arched his eyebrows and blew out a long breath. "Same here. I thought this day would never come."

When he slid into the Granada, the scent of the air freshener hit him, wiping out the pleasant feelings Heather's fragrance had stirred up, triggering a nauseous twinge instead. He removed it, wrapped it in a napkin, and then slipped it into the small garbage bag hanging from the cigarette lighter. "Am I the only one who feels sick from these things?"

"They give me a major headache," Heather said.

"Makes you wonder what sort of chemicals they have in them."

"Can't be good." Heather looked at the bag of food. "So, what's for dinner?"

"The usual." Sean held out a can of 7 Up. "Ham and Swiss cheese, right?"

Heather took a minute to react, her eyes fixed on the can of pop in Sean's hand. "How did you know that's what I like?"

"That's what you ordered last time."

Her eyes widened. "Geez, that was months ago!" She took the can.

Suddenly, Sean felt embarrassed about what he'd done. He kept quiet as he passed her the sandwich.

"That's very sweet of you. I can't believe you remembered."

As he felt his cheeks growing warm, Sean waved it off. "I have a good memory for these kinds of things."

"Merci beaucoup," Heather said, taking the sandwich, and when she saw Sean's confused look, she said, "That's French for 'thank you so much.'"

"You're taking French?"

"Oui."

"I'm French illiterate," Sean said. "But I had two years of Spanish in high school."

"Then I should say muchas gracias. That's the extent of my Spanish knowledge, though." She bit into her sandwich.

"De nada, señorita." Sean opened his can of root beer and held it up in a toasting gesture.

Heather popped open her 7 Up and bumped it against his can. "Cheers."

They both took a swig.

"May the force be with us," Sean added, hoping she wouldn't notice the jitteriness in his voice.

Heather nodded and took another bite. She chewed slowly and gazed out the windshield until she eventually said, "It's hard to believe this day is finally here."

Sean ran his hand through his hair and took a long inhale. "Totally."

They returned to silence. Sean nibbled sluggishly, forcing down each swallow, pushing himself to finish.

After a while, Heather said, "We lucked out with the weather, you know."

"Big time," Sean said emphatically. "This is as nice as we could hope for this time of year." Of course, he had worried all winter long about facing Thomas. But he'd also been fretting about what the weather would be like on this day. Bad weather could have screwed up his entire plan. There was good reason for concern, too. The old saying about March was, "In like a lion, out like a lamb," meaning early March tends to be winter-like, whereas the end of March is often spring-like. As it turned out, Heather was right: luck was on their side. What a relief.

"Especially considering how cold February was," Heather added.

"Yeah, that was rough." Ohio had been in a deep freeze for over a month, but the polar cold snap finally broke in the past week. "It's cloudy now, but they're not calling for rain."

Heather pointed to her unzipped coat. "I wore my warmest winter garb, but I might have overdressed."

Sean noticed she was wearing a Kent State sweatshirt underneath. He wondered if this meant anything, but he held back on asking. He covered his mouth with a napkin to catch any random spitfirings, and replied, "Maybe. It's not supposed to go anywhere near freezing tonight."

"Except we'll be sitting out there for a while. The cold has a way of wearing you down over time."

"That's so true." Sean thought about the time Karl's dad had taken the two of them hunting. Neither wanted to be there, but Mr. Wolf insisted. "You'll love it," he had told them. They didn't, though. What Sean remembered most from the outing was how warmly they believed they had dressed, yet they still felt frozen after just an hour.

As Sean's mind drifted back to Heather's Kent State sweatshirt, the lights went out in the doughnut shop. A short time later, Big Boy appeared in the doorway, wearing a jacket. He flipped the door sign to CLOSED and exited before locking the door behind him. He headed down the street and turned at the next block.

"The owner must live nearby," Heather said. "Wow, what a small town."

Sean forced down his last bite, then wiped his mouth on the napkin, just as his mother had always implored him to do. "You're wearing a Kent State sweatshirt."

She nodded. "It's official. That's where I'll be going."

Sean kept a stone face, but inside, he felt disappointment. He told himself he shouldn't be surprised. Did he really think Heather would end up at Ohio State if her boyfriend expected her to join him at Kent State? He tried to figure out how to respond, but the best he could do was change the subject. "The walkie-talkies are under your seat."

Heather leaned forward and fished them out. She passed one to him, then rolled the other over in her hands, examining it. "How do these things work?"

Sean explained all the controls, including the squelch knob, admitting he wasn't entirely sure he understood what it did. "Don't forget to let go of the TALK button when you're done speaking, or I won't be able to get through. I put new batteries in both, so we're all set."

Heather played with the buttons and dials for a while and then went back to her sandwich. After pushing the last piece into her mouth, she drummed her fingers on the armrest while she chewed. Eventually, she asked, "Are you wigging out?"

"I'm definitely on edge," Sean said, choosing the most understating words he could find. He turned and looked her in the eye. "But I can't wait to get this sonofabitch."

Heather pursed her lips and continued her fidgety finger-drumming. "I hope that's how it turns out. I can't help but worry, though. What if something goes wrong?"

The burial site loomed before them as Sean pulled the Granada into the cemetery parking spot. He forced himself to look away.

As if sharing his thoughts, Heather said, "God, I feel sick each time I see that thing."

Sean sighed. "I know the feeling." He killed the engine and pushed open his door.

Heather met him behind the car, pulling her woolen hat over her head. "Where's *your* hat?"

He responded with a smirk. "My campfire will keep *me* warm."

She let out a strained laugh. As she slipped her hands into her mittens, Heather cocked her head while her eyes darted around. "What's that eerie chirping sound?"

"Spring peeper frogs," Sean said. "They'll be even louder around sunset."

She turned to face the river. "How are we supposed to relax with that going on?"

"Funny thing about that..." Sean set off down the driveway, toward the river. "You only hear them on warm days this time of year in Ohio. But movie soundtracks always use this sound in nighttime scenes, no matter where the scene is supposed to be, or what time of year it is."

Heather gave him a playful smile. "That's something only biologists would notice."

Sean chuckled and passed her one of the walkie-talkies.

"There's something I keep wondering," Heather said, looking around. "Where should I watch for Thomas?"

Sean stopped, panned across their surroundings, and considered the question. He had pondered it many times. Was Thomas concealed somewhere within the cemetery? Could he be crawling out of a grave? The disturbed ground would be evident to the grounds crew, so probably not. Sean threw up his hands and started walking again. "Who knows?"

They turned onto the riverside road and slowly wandered toward Heather's hiding spot. "Maybe he's not coming *from* the cemetery," Heather said. "Maybe he's just passing *through.*"

Sean scanned the line of trees on either side of the cemetery grounds, then the row of houses along the back. "Could be. But one thing's for certain: if he's coming my way, he'll need to cross this road and the wall."

Heather rubbed her cheek with her mittened hand. "Yeah, so as long as I spot him when he goes over the wall, that's what matters."

"Exactly. And when you tell me he's heading my way, I'll roll out the red carpet."

Heather narrowed her eyes and studied Sean. "So, are you going to tell me your plan now?"

He grinned. "Why ruin the surprise?"

She let out a huff. "Do you think I'm comfortable being kept in the dark? Look, if we're going to be a team, you should tell me what's going on."

Sean puffed out his cheeks. He couldn't blame Heather for being uneasy. But he was the one who would be facing Thomas, while she'd be watching from a safe distance.

Chances were, if he tried to explain his plan in advance, she'd be shooting holes in it. But this was *going* to work. And when it did, he'd be hotdogging it. As nervous as he was now, he could hardly wait to see how impressed Heather would be. "Can you just trust me?"

She rolled her eyes and turned away.

"I promise it will all work out. Cross my heart." Sean traced a cross over his chest with his finger.

Heather continued to look away with a hardened expression.

"Hope to die. Stick a needle in my eye."

Her face softened. She chewed the inside of her cheek for a moment, then asked, "What comes after that?"

He scrunched his nose. "That's all I remember."

Heather furrowed her brow as if in deep thought, then shook her head. "So, anyway, Grand-Bob knows you're coming?"

He gave a thumbs-up. "He told me to park at the dead end and go on back."

As they approached the evergreen growing along the wall, Sean turned back to examine the perspective the location offered. "This is a perfect hiding spot."

"I'll say," Heather said, surveying her view. "If anything is heading for the river, I'll notice it, for sure."

She passed around the back of the evergreen and squeezed in between the branches and the wall. "Can you see me?"

Sean stood back and inspected the bush. "Barely, and I know where to look."

"Fantabulous." Heather extruded herself through the limbs. She glanced over the wall at the river. "Hey, is that ice?"

Sean leaned over and peered down. Ice floes drifted on the river's surface. "Yup. It was so cold this winter that parts of the river froze. The ice broke apart with the recent thaw, so the current is carrying chunks downstream."

Heather turned her attention to the walkie-talkie. "Let's test these things." She freed one hand from her mitten and rotated the volume dial, clicking it away from the OFF position, before pulling out the antenna.

Sean powered his unit on and turned away. As he crossed the road, he spoke into the device, "Breaker one-nine, do you read me?"

"What the heck does that mean?" Heather's voice came through, loud and clear.

Sean laughed. "I have no clue. But they said it in that 'Convoy' song."

"I always hated that tune," Heather declared from across the road, forgoing the walkie-talkie.

"You brought a flashlight?" Sean asked, heading back toward her.

She pulled it out of her coat pocket, switched it on, and pointed it at him.

Sean shielded the glare of the light with his hand. "You're all set, then. Remember, if you get in any kind of trouble, jet back to your car." He pointed in the direction of the town square.

As he turned toward his car, Heather asked, "What about you?"

He froze. The uneasiness he'd been suppressing burst free, flooding his mind. *Yeah. What about* me?

Sean swallowed, forced a smile, and took a step across the roadway. "I've got this. Don't worry about me."

Chapter 10

Sean pulled his backpack out of the trunk and slung it over his shoulder. He lifted the bundle of firewood and balanced it on one arm, then used his free hand to close the trunk, leaving behind his basket of dirty laundry as the sole remaining occupant.

While trudging up the driveway, he caught sight of Grand-Bob standing in his front window, waving with one hand and holding a bottle in the other. With his arms full, Sean responded with a chin lift before heading between the mobile home and the detached garage, making a beeline for the open farm field behind the house.

The backpack's load was barely noticeable, but the bundle of firewood was awkward to carry. As he made his way across the field, he kept shifting it in his arms to lessen the growing burning sensation in his muscles.

The closer Sean got to the river, the louder the spring peeper frogs' chirping calls became. *Heather was right,* he thought. *They do sound sort of eerie.*

As he approached the end of the cultivated soil, he scanned the ground for the blackened circle. When he spotted it, he dropped the bundle and slipped out of the backpack. He removed the walkie-talkie and carried it over to the bank.

The AC/DC ticket stubs remained where he'd left them, affixed to the tree with now-rusty thumbnails, frayed and faded beyond recognition.

Sean turned on the walkie-talkie and pressed the talk button. "Breaker one-nine, do you read me?"

After a brief burst of static, Heather responded, "I still don't know what that means."

Sean laughed nervously. "Me neither."

He side-stepped along the bank, seeking a gap between the trees for the best view of the evergreen. When he found it, he waved. Heather's blue jacketed arm popped out of the bush and waved back.

"I couldn't see you at all until you waved."

"Stellar. I just hope Thomas doesn't have some supernatural sixth sense."

"Most definitely." Sean checked his watch. It was 6:40. "I'd better start this fire before it gets completely dark. Be careful over there."

"Ten-four, good buddy." Heather giggled, and then the walkie-talkie went silent.

With a shake of his head, he began collecting fallen tree branches for kindling.

In the middle of the charcoal remnants, Sean stacked the smallest limbs, forming something like a miniature version of the second little pig's stick house, just as he'd learned in Boy Scouts. When the stack was tall enough that it threatened to topple over, he propped larger sticks above it, forming a teepee with plenty of gaps to let in the air. He set aside the larger branches to continue feeding the fire.

Pulling two half-gallon cans of Kingsford Sure-Fire lighter fluid from the backpack, Sean set one aside and twisted the other's plastic cap open. He sprinkled some fluid over the branch structure, placed the can with its mate, struck a match, and dropped it onto the wood. The flame jumped in size, then spread over the kindling, engulfing it within seconds.

As the wood burned, he added more branches, until the flames rose to waist height. He opened the bundle of wood he'd brought in his trunk and added four split logs to the fire.

"Hey, breaker one-nine, that's quite an inferno you've got going over there."

Sean picked up the walkie-talkie and pressed the talk button. "Never mind that, good buddy. You're supposed to be watching *that* side of the river."

"The coast is clear so far. Over and out."

Sean smiled. Sifting through the backpack, he located the hand hoe, which he carried to the riverbank's edge. He got down on his hands and knees and went to work, gouging a shallow one-foot-wide trench along the bank.

The task went quickly, since the soil was soft and not frozen, and the trench he was digging was only two inches deep. Before long, he judged he'd gone sixty feet. At that point, he curved the trench away from the bank, following an arc, until it was heading straight out from the riverbank. When that segment was twenty feet long, he turned the trench back in. Before long, he had formed an elongated oval.

Next, he dug a segment of trench extending from the center of the oval toward the fire but ending a few paces short. By the time he was finished, the sky was full-on dark, and the campfire needed more wood.

Sean warmed his hands over the fire, then tended to it. As he added logs, he tried to gauge whether he had enough to last a few more hours. Because he couldn't be sure, he searched out a couple more fallen limbs from the riverbank, which he dragged back to the fire and laid beside the woodpile.

The sky had darkened completely, although the clouds were thin enough to let some moonlight shine through. The chorus of spring peepers had grown in volume, giving the nightscape that eerie movie-like vibe—except *this* was real.

Sean removed a box of heavy-duty aluminum foil from the backpack and carried it to the oval. He dropped back to his knees and went about lining the shallow trench with the tinfoil, molding the material to fit the trench's shape and hold it in place. Working in the dark was slow going, and Sean was extra careful to avoid punching holes in the foil.

After the oval trench and its extension segment were fully lined, he stirred the fire, added a few more pieces of wood, and then rewarmed his hands over the revived blaze.

Next, Sean took the tarp from the backpack and unrolled it near the fire. Removing three Roman candles from the bag, he tucked them under the back edge of the tarp, shielding them from stray embers that might pop that way.

When he looked at his watch, it was already 8:30. *Heather's been out there for almost two hours. You should check on her.*

Sean picked up the walkie-talkie and strolled over to the riverbank. The evergreen bush had become little more than a shadowy smudge. Beyond it, the oldest section of the graveyard had fallen into murky silhouettes, as still as a landscape painting. The ancient tombstones leaned every which way, like a mouthful of crooked teeth. He shuddered, turned his gaze to Heather's hiding spot, and pressed the Talk button. "Hey, good buddy, everything okay over there?"

"Getting a little chilly, just sitting here. What've you been up to?"

"Rolling out that red carpet. Pretty well set now. Any sign of the boogeyman boy?"

"Nope. All's quiet over here. It's like a cemetery or something." Heather gave an apprehensive laugh. "It's really creepy now."

"Yeah, I bet." Sean wanted to say something comforting, but came up empty. "Well, it won't be long now. He should show up within an hour."

"That's exactly what I'm afraid of."

He wished Heather wasn't over there all by herself. "Pay attention and keep still," he reminded her. "And be careful!"

Sean knew, however, that it was *he* in the line of fire.

At the fire, Sean grabbed the opened Kingsford can and carried it to the foil-lined oval. He tilted the jug over and squeezed, spraying a stream of lighter fluid into the trench, letting it puddle generously. The noxious smell of the flammable liquid made him feel woozy, so he tried to squirt it from the furthest distance possible as he followed along the oval.

After the fluid ran out when he had covered about three-fourths of the foil, he opened the second can to complete the task, using about half of it by the time he covered everything.

Once finished, Sean stretched out beside the fire, his back facing the flames, using a trick he'd learned in Boy Scouts: if you're at a campfire watching for something, turn away from the fire so the light won't blind you. He scanned the trees along the riverbank, watching for the slightest sign of movement in the shadows, but all remained still. It was a calm night, so even the tree limbs barely moved.

As the minutes passed, Sean increasingly felt all alone. With nothing to do but think, he gazed up at the sky, watching as clouds drifted across, letting through occasional glimpses of the moon and stars. Two years had passed since that night with Karl. Now, Sean was back. He'd been waiting months for this night, and after all that time, here he was. What was he in for? There was no telling.

Eventually, the fire dwindled, so Sean got up to stoke it. He stared at Grand-Bob's house across the field, watching as the television light flickered beyond the curtains. Would Grand-Bob see what was about to happen? *Nah, he's probably already passed out.*

Although his tension level was rising steadily, Sean forced himself to stretch back out beside the fire. He cracked his knuckles and fought the urge to check the time. *You should've brought your Walkman.* No, he needed to be able to hear. But so far, there were no sounds except the spring peepers' mating calls. Even that had waned as the clock ticked into full-fledged nighttime.

Before long, the fire died down again. When he got up to feed it more wood, he allowed himself to look at his watch. It was almost 9:30. *But still, no Thomas.*

He examined the walkie-talkie and confirmed it was on, then scolded himself for even questioning whether he might have accidentally switched it off. *Should I check in with Heather?* They had agreed to remain quiet unless needed. *Maybe she fell asleep, though.* He scoffed at the idea. *She's too nervous...and probably too cold.* He told himself to be patient, stretched out over the tarp, and resumed his wait.

The next time Sean looked at his watch, it was just after 9:45. Was it time to worry? He pushed himself up from the tarp and added the last log to the fire, then the extra branches he had gathered. That was it for the firewood.

As the campfire consumed the new fuel, he stared toward the river. After a few minutes, he picked up the walkie-talkie and headed to the bank, skirting around the foil-lined trench. Following along the slope's edge in the opposite direction of the drifting ice floes, Sean watched the still silhouettes in the graveyard as they slid past one another with his shifting vantage point.

He wandered to a point directly across the river from the evergreen and dropped into a sitting position. The bush appeared deserted. He narrowed his eyes and leaned forward, studying the stillness of it, questioning whether she was even there. *Of course she is.* But how could he be so sure? Maybe he should call her on the walkie-talkie, just in case. *Don't be a dipshit. She's hiding.*

His eyes ticked to the cemetery, and he rolled his gaze slowly across the grounds, watching for the slightest movement amongst the vast sea of headstones and beyond.

Bubbles breaking on the water's surface amidst ice floes caught Sean's attention. He stiffened and eyed that spot on Heather's side of the river, a little way downstream from the evergreen. As he watched them, he realized the bubbles were moving, heading toward the middle of the river. Then a V-shaped wake formed, the ripples expanding as its source moved across the river. *Was it an animal? A beaver, maybe?*

When the animal broke the surface, Sean's breath caught. A frantic voice inside his head blurted out, *That's no beaver!*

The crown of a head rose out of the water. As water streamed off the hair, the eyes blinked open. Sean jerked backward. Those monstrous red eyes that had appeared in his nightmares over the past two years glared out from gaunt sockets, gleaming in the black of the night.

When Sean jumped to his feet, his movement caught Thomas's attention. He promptly veered in Sean's direction, maneuvering between floating chunks of ice drifting with the current. His nose, then his mouth, emerged from the water.

Unable to wrench his shocked gape away, Sean staggered backward, his heart jackhammering as if it might burst from his chest.

Why haven't you heard from Heather?

Thomas closed in on the shore, rising steadily. The turtle shell hanging from his neck appeared when his chest cleared the surface. Water sheeted off his torso as he propelled himself by foot over the last shallow stretch.

Sean turned and bolted, pressing the walkie-talkie against his mouth. "Are you there?"

As the seconds ticked by with no response, Sean's mind launched into a full-blown panic.

Chapter 11

Sean raced toward the fire, resisting the urge to call again, knowing if he pushed the talk button, he might miss Heather's response. He was halfway there when a burst of static came through, followed by her voice. "I'm still here."

"Do you see him?" he gasped back.

Heather took another moment to respond. "No."

How could she not see him? Then it dawned on Sean that she probably could not see the river from her hiding spot.

"He's on my side of the river!"

After a pause, Heather shrieked, "Oh, my God! He's climbing the bank. How did I miss him? I was watching!"

When it suddenly clicked, Sean blurted, "He came *out* of the river!" He took the last few steps to the campfire. "I need to go now."

As he chucked the walkie-talkie into the backpack, he heard Heather's muffled voice yell, "Be careful, Sean!"

Grabbing one of the Roman candles from under the tarp, Sean stood sentry with his winded chest heaving, the fire positioned behind him to preserve his vision.

The horrible sound of sloshing took him back to that night with Karl. With clenched teeth, he strained to get a read on the direction of the noise. Moments later, a featureless form lumbered out of the trees, sending Sean's heart leaping into his throat.

The figure took shape as it plodded closer, water pouring from its tattered clothes, its pallid gray skin glistening in the night. The red eyes locked on Sean with a burning glare.

Sean wanted to flee, but he told himself to hold his ground. He used his free hand to feel the tip of the Roman candle, confirming he had it pointed with the fuse out. He stepped backward, pivoting to face the fire, timing his movement with Thomas's lurching forward progress.

The tinfoil crinkled—the sound Sean had been waiting for. He held the Roman candle in the flames, and when he heard the fuse fizzle, he raised the stick with both hands and pointed it at his target.

Pop. The candle recoiled as the first ball of fire shot out of the end, burning so brightly that Sean had to squint. The shooting ball flew well over Thomas's head and emitted a crackling sound as it extinguished in the band of trees.

Sean aimed lower. *Pop.* The next ball of fire shot to one side of Thomas, but didn't seem to faze him as he tramped closer.

Sean lowered the stick further. *Pop.* The third ball of fire hit the dirt one foot away from the leading segment of the trench, bounced past Thomas, and sizzled out on the embankment.

Adjusting his aim slightly higher, Sean waited. *Pop.* The fourth ball of fire hit the end of the segment, skipped up, and into Thomas, who brushed it away like a bothersome fly.

Sean groaned. Why hadn't the fireball ignited the lighter fluid? He had one more shot before his entire plan fell apart.

But then his eyes adjusted, and he noticed a flame scooting down the length of the segment, spreading from the spot where the fireball had bounced. The flame split into two as it zipped along the oval, racing to reconnect on the opposite side. Soon, the entire oval was alight, turning the scene into daylight. Sean felt a surge of euphoria. Everything was falling into place.

As Thomas studied the fire surrounding him, Sean aimed the Roman candle at him. *Pop.* The fifth and final shot hit Thomas squarely in the chest. Thomas staggered backward as the fireball fell to the ground before extinguishing in its final crackling burst. Thomas righted himself and glowered at Sean.

"Bulls-eye!" Sean whooped. "Take that, you sonofabitch! There's more where that came from!"

Heather began blurting indecipherably on the walkie-talkie, her voice muffled beyond comprehension with the speaker ensconced within the backpack.

Sean pitched the spent Roman candle into the fire and lunged for the can of lighter fluid.

He and Karl had been skilled pyromaniacs during the era of their youth before they moved on to drug experimentation. So, Sean knew that if he used the right amount of pressure, he could squirt lighter fluid straight into the fire, fueling the blaze like a makeshift flame-thrower, yet not allowing the fire to carry back to the can. With this in mind, Sean rushed toward the burning ring.

A wall of heat stopped him in his tracks. He covered his face with his sleeve and jumped back to a safer distance.

After recovering from the heat blast, Sean turned the plastic cap to release it. He raised the can, tilted it forward, pointed it at Thomas, and squeezed, sending a liquid stream his way. The stream fell in an arc, but short of the burning oval. Sean raised the can, adjusted the angle, and squeezed harder. This time, the stream reached the oval, sending roaring flames into the air, but still short of Thomas.

Sean yelled, "Shit!" and tried to press forward. But the heat was too intense. He retreated, dropped the can on the ground, and lunged for the Roman candles instead. After tossing one beside the lighter fluid can, he took hold of the other, orienting it with the fuse end facing outward.

Thomas leered at Sean from behind the wall of fire with enraged, red eyes as he stumped forward.

Sean moved the tip of the Roman candle toward the campfire while Thomas lumbered closer. But when he stepped near the flaming trench, his foot covering, which had apparently been wetted with the fuel, burst into flames.

Before the Roman candle fuse caught, Sean pulled it away from the fire.

With flames licking up his leg, Thomas looked down, then wheeled around to face the river. The grotesque head wound that had seared itself into Sean's darkest memories came into full view.

Thomas hurried away, but when he stepped through the far end of the oval, he planted his other foot in the trench and came out with fire covering it, too. With flames dancing up both legs, Thomas shambled toward the river.

As Sean hustled around the flaming oval, he heard Heather yelling. He glanced across the river and cringed. She had wriggled out from the evergreen hiding place and climbed onto the wall. Although he wished she had remained hidden, he couldn't exactly blame her—the turmoil she was surely getting glimpses of would be shocking.

Sean stopped, held the Roman candle over the flaming trench, and when the fuse caught, he spun around and pointed it at Thomas's back. *Pop!* The fireball launched and hit him between the shoulders, dropping behind him before sizzling out. Paying no heed, Thomas tromped down the riverbank on burning feet.

Pop! The second ball also hit him squarely in the back. He stumbled down the slope toward the water, leaving a smoky wake behind.

Sean gagged on a whiff of what he imagined scorched, rotten meat might smell like.

Pop! The third ball ricocheted off one tree into another, then dropped to the ground.

Thomas's descent down the embankment became an out-of-control tumble into the water. As the water doused his flaming legs, steam billowed up around him. He toppled over and disappeared below the surface.

Sean kept the firework stick pointed at the river. *Pop!* The fourth ball shot straight into the water, right where Thomas had plunged, extinguishing it without the usual sizzle.

Heather yelled, "What are you doing?" She was standing on the wall now.

Pop! The fifth and final ball followed the same trace, glancing off an ice floe before falling harmlessly into the water near the middle of the river.

Sean hung onto the Roman candle shell as if reluctant to admit it was spent, but he didn't respond to Heather. He nudged forward until the bank fell off sharply, and squinted, studying the spot in the river where Thomas had disappeared. He waited and watched, but saw nothing.

He got away, Sean told himself, shaking his head in defeat. *The bastard got away.*

After a long stretch of stunned silence, Heather yelled from across the river, "So, *that* was your grand plan?"

Sean let out a sigh of exasperation. He turned to face the flaming oval, which had diminished to a bluish shimmer, and tossed the spent Roman candle into the center.

His brain stuttered as he tried to formulate how to mount his defense. This wasn't how he'd imagined things going. If everything had gone as planned, Thomas would have been a pile of smoldering ash at the edge of the field by now. Instead, Thomas had escaped.

"Now I see why you didn't want to tell me," Heather said.

Sean stared at her shadow, trying to discern whether she was teasing him, or truly angry. Probably the latter. His plan had failed miserably, so she had every right to feel that way. He had envisioned Heather being impressed with him. Instead, she most likely thought he was an idiot.

As she lowered herself into a sitting position, Heather's knee bumped the walkie-talkie, knocking it off the wall. She switched on her flashlight, leaned over, and scanned the slope. The light beam settled on the walkie-talkie, resting on the gravel a few feet below the base of the stone structure.

"Just leave it," Sean yelled with his hands cupped around his mouth.

Heather gazed down at the river as if questioning whether Thomas was gone.

"It's okay! Just leave it!" Sean yelled again.

Instead, she turned off the flashlight, pocketed it, slid forward, and dropped onto the gravel. Bracing herself by holding onto the top of the wall, she reached down with one hand and grabbed the walkie-talkie. The instant she placed it on the wall, a dark mass sprang from the water directly beneath her.

Sean flinched. Terror erupted in his mind as he took in the sight of Thomas clambering up the slope.

Heather attempted to pull herself back onto the wall, but her footing gave out, and she slid down the embankment several feet, losing her grasp on the top of the structure.

Without even thinking, Sean rushed down the riverbank, grabbing a series of trees to slow his descent, bouncing down to the river's edge in what could best be described as a controlled fall. He caught himself on a tree trunk just before he would have hurtled into the water.

As he stripped off his jacket, he glimpsed Heather attempting to pull herself up. But she seemed to slide downward an equal distance for every movement upward. Meanwhile, Thomas had scaled up the gravel slope by a body length.

Sean threw his jacket on the slope and stepped off the bank into the icy water. Dropping waist-deep on the first step, the rush of cold almost took his breath away. He clenched his jaw and took another small pace forward. His foot slid out of his tennis shoe, which remained stuck in the mud at the river's bottom, and the water promptly rose to his chest, his heart seizing with the shock of it. On the next pace, he lost the bottom completely, and his other shoe, as well.

Sean began dog paddling, but his clothing weighed him down, dragging against his movements. A large ice floe drifted in front of him, and as he adjusted his angle to let it pass, he wondered what the temperature of the water was. It was obviously above freezing, but considering the chunks of ice floating on the surface, it couldn't be much warmer.

The frigid water caused a burning pain on his skin. Gasping for breath, he fought to keep his head above the surface, fixing his attention on the opposite bank.

As Sean paddled, he looked up at Heather, who now appeared considerably further away. He realized the current was carrying him downriver. She was still struggling to get a foothold on the gravel while Thomas had climbed one-third of the way up.

Sean looked back at the bank he was trying to reach. It still seemed no closer. Was he even making progress? He told himself not to think that way. *Keep going!*

But as the seconds ticked by, the near-frozen water seemed to be sucking the warmth out of his body. It felt as though thousands of tiny knives were stabbing his limbs. He found himself barely able to breathe, almost like the wind had been knocked out of him.

A massive ice floe came his way, and he considered grabbing hold of it, using it as a life preserver while he regained control of his lungs. Instead, he let it pass and fought to kick harder, propelling himself forward with all his might.

As his stiff limbs flailed underwater, he looked up the bank and caught a glimpse of Thomas, who was now over halfway to the top. Thankfully, Heather seemed to have found her footing and had her hands back on the wall.

When Sean turned his attention back to his struggle to cross the river, it occurred to him he was moving downstream faster than he was closing in on the other side. Worse yet, his arms and legs had turned so numb, he could no longer even tell if they were doing what he needed them to. Except, his head was bobbing on the surface, so this seemed to indicate his limbs were still at work, right? *Keep going!*

he told himself, repeating it in a chant. *Keep going! Keep going! Keep going!*

As another chunk of ice drifted by, he peeked back at Heather. She was even further away, but the good news was she was mounting the wall. The bad news was Thomas would soon be within reach of her. Sean wanted to yell, to warn her, but there was no way he could muster the voice. She *had* to know Thomas was closing in, though.

Suddenly realizing he had no sensation whatsoever in his limbs, for the first time, Sean comprehended the grave danger *he* was in. *Is this how I die?* And just like that, his thoughts veered from saving Heather to fighting for his own survival.

For a fleeting instant, he considered turning around, until a backward glance told him he was well past the halfway point. That was when Sean realized he was no longer so far from Heather's side. But without feeling in his arms or legs, the notion of reaching the shore seemed impossible.

What would dying be like? Maybe it was nothing to fear. Would they find his body downstream, tangled up in a tree like Marilyn Warner's? Or would scavenger wildlife pick his bones clean before anyone discovered his remains?

Sean recognized he was losing the will to fight. But did he care?

You need to *care!* He ordered his arms and legs to keep moving. Since he couldn't feel them, all he could do was blindly trust they were obeying. *Keep going!*

The weight of his clothing dragged him down, and he soon inhaled a splash of water. He tried but failed to cough it out, his diaphragm merely spasming in vain.

As his mindset vacillated between panic and surrender, Sean heard a voice. "Can you touch the bottom?"

It was Karl's voice.

"You should be close enough now."

Sean gave a few more feeble coughs onto the water's surface and turned his eyes to the riverbank. Sure enough, Karl was propped on the gravel, his legs bent, and his forearms resting casually on his knees. The bedcover he'd worn to the hospital hung over him.

"Try it," Karl said.

Sean told his legs to check. Unable to feel them, he couldn't know if they followed his order. But he soon felt a jarring sensation in his torso. A tidal wave of relief crashed over him. He still had feeling in his midsection, so he wasn't fully paralyzed, after all. *Not yet, at least.*

"Told you so," Karl said.

It was Karl, alright. He *loved* saying those three words. But he was gone now. The gravel slope was completely vacant, as though he'd never been there at all.

Pressing down into the underwater bank's muddy incline and leaning forward, Sean commanded his other foot to take a step. The gap between him and the embankment narrowed further.

Fueled by his dwindling adrenaline, Sean pushed with all his might, losing his socks to the muck as he thrust himself forward. The water became shallower as he slipped and staggered across the remaining few feet. He collapsed onto the gravel embankment, numb to the impact.

Tapping the last of his energy, he crawled up the slope a short distance, far enough to extract his feet from the river. He crumpled on the graveled slope and tucked into a fetal position, his body trembling violently.

Yet despite his uncontrollable shuddering, he no longer felt cold. In fact, he felt *warm.* How could that be? *Maybe you're dead already,* Sean thought to himself. *That might explain why you saw Karl.*

But Sean was pretty certain he hadn't died, so he focused on voiding the water from his lungs. He coughed and gagged, working out a few drops each time, until the wrenching feeling in his chest had mostly subsided.

As he lay there gasping, he peered up the slope just in time to see Thomas lunge for Heather. She was on top of the wall now, and she met his advance with a solid kick to the chest, sending him flailing backward.

Thomas hung there for a moment, his arms pinwheeling as he tottered. He flopped on his back, then rolled down the rest of the bank before splashing into the water.

To Sean, the entire sequence played out like a dream. When it was over, the hypothermic strain on his body overtook him. He closed his eyes and succumbed to exhaustion.

Chapter 12

SEAN'S NEXT THOUGHT FRAGMENT was hearing what sounded like popcorn popping. *Jiffy Pop.*

No, that's not right. As he clawed his way back to consciousness, he remembered where he was, and realized he was hearing a landslide of gravel sweeping down the slope.

The next thing that came to mind was, *It's Thomas. He's coming for me.* But it couldn't be; Thomas had fallen into the river—Heather had knocked him there.

So, what was sliding down the slope? The stone avalanche crescendoed and then tapered off. "Sean, are you okay?" It was Heather.

He pried open his eyes and saw a form crawling across the gravel bank toward him.

How long was he out? It could have been twenty seconds or twenty minutes. It was impossible to tell.

Sean tried to respond but couldn't. He had no idea how to answer her question. His teeth chattered so furiously that he wondered if they might come loose. And the bone-chilling coldness had returned. Maybe that was a good sign. But certainly, he couldn't be okay, could he?

A stray stone plunked into his forehead, and the shot of pain he felt seemed to clear his confusion. He rubbed his forehead and realized he had regained feeling in his arms. Maybe he wasn't going to die after all.

Heather pushed onto her feet, angling them into the gravel to catch hold, while leaning into the slope with one hand. Inching closer until she was within reach, she dropped to her hip beside him. She switched on the flashlight, swept the beam over him a few times, then turned it back off.

"Can you hear me?"

Sean nodded.

"You could have drowned! Or died of hypothermia!" Heather pulled her hat off and shimmied it onto his head.

"Let's get this wet shirt off." She began peeling off his sweatshirt. "You can wear my coat."

Sean tried to assist, but it was hard controlling his trembling arms. When Heather finally got the sweatshirt off, she began stripping off his thermal undershirt. Normally, he would have been self-conscious about his skinny build, but after his utter failure to destroy Thomas or to save Heather, he had little dignity left.

It was strange how it somehow felt less cold with his upper body exposed. Heather wrapped her coat around him, helping guide his arms into the sleeves. Next, she slipped her mittens over his clenched fists.

When Heather began pulling off her boots, Sean asked, "What are you doing?" He struggled to form the words with his teeth chattering and his mouth numb, so it came out sounding more like "wear-your-dune."

"You're going to look so cute in my socks."

"I can't take your socks."

She pulled them over his feet, anyway. "You're lucky. I wore my thick woolen pair. Extra cozy."

The chill had settled too deep in his bones for Sean to feel warm in the dry clothing. But at least the violent shivers had diminished. "Here's a tip," he said as she crawled back up beside him. "Don't go swimming this time of year."

Heather laughed and hugged him. "I thought you were a goner."

Sean was disappointed when she pulled away. "I thought the same about you. But you kicked that bastard's ass!"

Heather made like The Incredible Hulk, flexing her arms and letting out a little roar. "You're pretty tough yourself. Not many people would have made it across that ice river!"

Sean gave a weak, teeth-chattering smile. He rolled up into a crouch, pressed his mittened fists against his mouth, and blew into them, warming his fingers with his breath. The truth was, he'd only made it with the assist from Karl's mirage—which he *wouldn't* mention. "It was stupid."

Heather didn't respond, which he took as her agreement.

As she wrung the water out of his clothes, Sean scanned the river for signs of movement. Even during daylight, most of the water was too deep, too murky to see the bottom. Now, in the darkness of the night, there was zero chance of seeing anything lurking under the surface.

Heather glanced at the water. "Let's get out of here. We need to get you someplace warm, anyway."

"I need to go back to the fire. Get my stuff and clean up."

Heather craned her neck and looked up the slope. "Do you think you can climb up?"

Sean avoided looking back, feeling like he might be discouraged by what he saw. "Yeah."

Heather pushed onto her feet, draped his wet shirts over her neck, and held out a hand. He took it with his mittened hands and stood with her help. He took a minute to steady himself and gather the strength in his legs, then released her hand and turned to face the slope. “I can do this,” he said, wondering if he was assuring Heather, or himself.

They scaled the graveled bank side-by-side, using their hands to lean into the incline. Each step up led to a backward slide, so it took two paces of effort for every single pace of progress. In his lightheaded state, Sean had to take a dozen breaks along the way. He was grateful for the socks, though. Trying to climb on bare, frozen feet would have been impossible.

When they eventually reached the top, Sean propped himself against the stonework to recover. Although he was starting to feel himself again, the climb had been daunting after what his body had been through.

Heather hopped onto the wall, grabbed her walkie-talkie, and wheeled her legs over the other side. “I’ll run to my car. You wait here.”

Sean looked down at the river. “No way.”

She chuckled as she dropped to the ground. “Good point. Can’t blame you there.”

After a minute’s rest, Sean climbed over the wall and they set off on the most direct route to the Chevette, through the cemetery. They walked silently as they passed the mass burial site, the faint candlelight flickering inside the hanging lantern.

Heather switched on her flashlight, lighting a path through the swath of headstones. When they reached the back end of the grounds, they followed a walkway into the residential block, where streetlights illuminated the sidewalk. "Glad to get out of there," she whispered, turning off her light.

One block further, Heather said, "I'll jog ahead to start my car. Get a head start on warming it up," and she took off.

When Sean turned onto the deserted town square, he spotted her rummaging through the Chevette's cargo area as vapor billowed from the tailpipe. Upon hearing his footsteps, she held up a pair of work gloves and boots. "These are my dad's. Too bad he didn't have a pair of pants stashed in there."

"This is great," Sean said, taking the gloves and boots. "But I'm all set on the pants. I've got a laundry basket full of dirty clothes in my trunk."

They piled into the car and Heather drove a block off the town square, parking in front of the library with the engine running. When the air streaming from the vents became hot, Heather turned the fan dial to HIGH and steered the vents in Sean's direction. He leaned into them and rubbed his hands over the warmth.

Heather waited and watched, chewing her lip. After a while, she asked, "Is it okay if I go with you?"

"For sure. Grand-Bob probably passed out hours ago." He looked at his watch, which read 10:05, and switched his eyes to the clock on the dashboard, which read 10:30. Sean pointed to it. "Is this right?"

Heather nodded.

Sean blew a raspberry at his watch. "It's supposed to be waterproof."

Heather tapped her fingers nervously on the steering wheel. "Are you feeling any warmer?"

"A little." Although he was still chilled to the core, the uncontrollable shivering had ended. "I need to get out of these wet pants, though. Let's get going."

Heather kept the blower on full blast. She drove slowly, which Sean figured she was doing to give him more time in the heat. He appreciated the gesture, but part of him just wanted to get back to Clarkton, into his bed, with his heating blanket turned on high.

When the Granada's taillights flashed a reflective red glow at the gravel road's dead end, Heather turned off the Chevette's headlights. She coasted the rest of the way and tucked in beside his parked car. "You can change into dry pants in here. I'll keep the engine running so you still have heat."

After Sean added several layers of dry, albeit ready-for-the-wash clothing, they headed across the field, toward the fading glow of the campfire's dying embers. The night had fallen silent, the last of the spring peepers having retired with the others.

Halfway across the field, Heather broke the silence. "Something tells me we haven't seen the last of Thomas."

"Me too," Sean said.

"But at least we prevented someone else from dying this year."

"Yeah, there's that," Sean said, thinking, *Even if you fell flat on your face in the process.* He rubbed his cheek with the open palm of Heather's dad's work glove. "I keep wondering, where did he go?"

"He went where he came from."

Sean nodded. "The river. I always assumed that when Thomas came to our campfire, he came from somewhere *across* the river. But it turns out he came *from* the river."

"That would explain why Jack first saw him near the stone wall."

"And your mother..."

Heather drew in a deep, hitching breath. "Maybe when she went near that wall..."

A scene surfaced in Sean's imagination of what Heather had left unsaid: Marilyn Warner, alone at night, approaching the wall.

Thomas, lunging out from the shadows, snatching her, dragging her over. Down she went, into the river, never to surface alive. It all would have happened within seconds.

And tonight, Heather narrowly escaped the same fate.

The awful visualization faded as they approached the glowing coals of the fire. Heather looked over the scene while Sean rearranged the remaining stubs of firewood on the embers so they'd burn away.

Under the light of the newly kindled flames, Sean went to work. He gathered the items he'd brought and stuffed them in the backpack, fetched the spent Roman candle from inside the oval where he had tossed it, and deposited it in the flames.

Next, Sean began collecting the tinfoil from the oval trench. Heather joined him, working from the opposite end. They each wadded up the used foil into a ball, which grew into the size of two basketballs by the time they were finished. Sean stepped on the two tinfoil balls to squish them down, then crammed them into the backpack and headed toward the tree line.

"I left my jacket down by the river, and over here..." Sean stopped in his tracks.

"What is it?" Heather asked.

He scratched his head, scanning the ground. "I left them right here."

"Left what?"

"A can of lighter fluid and an unused Roman candle." He walked in a small circle, his eyes glued to the ground, then doubled back, shaking his head. "They were *right here!*" Sean stopped, turned, and glared at the river. "And now, they're *gone.*"

Chapter 13

The Homer Reporter's front-page headline screamed at Sean. His heart began racing as he stared at it, the words striking him like a sledgehammer against his forehead.

Two Dead in Moravian Village
Arson Suspected

Pressing a fist against his mouth, Sean unfolded the paper with his other hand and spread it over the kitchen table. He inhaled a long, quivering breath and forced himself to read the article.

> ***By DM Guay,*** *Staff Reporter*
>
> MORAVIAN VILLAGE – A couple who died in a fatal house fire have been identified as Donald Harden, 66, and Betty Harden, 63, according to the Homer County Sheriff's Office.
>
> Volunteer firefighters responded to a report of a house fire in the 200 block of S. Hickory Street at

> 11:32 p.m. Friday, after a call from a neighbor. Crews arrived at the scene to find fire engulfing the first and second floors of the residence. After the fire was contained, Betty and Donald Harden were found unresponsive in an upstairs bedroom and pronounced dead at the scene, according to Kerry Bryan, the Moravian Village Fire Chief. The preliminary cause of death is smoke inhalation, pending an investigation by the Homer County Coroner.
>
> The cause of the fire is unknown, although a witness reported seeing Fire Chief Bryan collecting an empty can of accelerant and a spent firework shell at the scene.

No, no, no! Sean flipped the paper over, as though concealing the headline might make this thing go away. He sidestepped the table and faced the front window, staring blindly into the distance as he waited for his pulse to settle.

The foolishness of having believed they'd averted another killing sunk in.

Then, the words "can of accelerant" and "spent firework shell" began ringing in his head. His knees weakened. He grabbed the window frame to steady himself. *You had a hand in this, didn't you?*

But wait...

The world began spinning as Sean's brain connected a couple more dots, and distress gave way to panic. *Shit!* Just when Sean thought things could not get any worse, they did.

Anxious to escape Homer County, Sean told his parents he would return to campus to study. He fueled up at the gas station before getting on the interstate, and when he went inside to pay, he picked up his own copy of The Homer Reporter, folding it over to conceal the dreadful headline.

With the paper tucked under his arm, he headed to the pay phone on the edge of the parking area. He dug a bag of coins from his pocket and a scrap of paper from his wallet. After dialing the number, he fished out the quarters and fed them into the payphone to fund the long-distance call.

"Hello?"

Sean's shoulders relaxed a notch when Heather was the one who picked up on the other end. "Hey there."

"Oh, hey, are you feeling better?"

"Yeah...well, no. I'm not cold anymore. That's the good news."

Heather took a moment to respond. "What's the bad news?"

Sean read the newspaper article to her while she listened in silence. When he finished, he could almost hear the angst in her breathing. He folded the paper up and pressed his open hand over his eyes.

"Holy crap," Heather eventually said, slowly and quietly.

"You can say that again."

"Now we know what happened to your lighter fluid and that Roman candle."

"Yeah, but guess whose fingerprints were on them?"

Sean spent the next few days lying low, sweating it out each time the phone rang. Since most of the incoming calls were for his dorm roommate anyway, he had already been in the habit of not answering the phone. Now, more than ever, Sean made a point of it.

On Thursday, six days after the fire, he got the first indication of what he'd been bracing himself for.

"Yeah, he's here," the roommate said into the phone. "Just a minute." He covered the receiver with his palm and whispered to Sean, "It's some old guy."

Sean immediately assumed it was someone from the Homer County Sheriff's Office. His heart launched into a rapid-fire hammering as he took the handset.

"Hello?"

"Howdy, Buttercup."

Sean's tension ebbed slightly with the sound of Grand-Bob's voice. Even so, why would he be calling? How did he even get the number?

Then, Sean remembered he had given it to him when he'd arranged the "memorial campfire."

"Hi, Grand-Bob."

"Listen, this call is probably costing me a fortune, so we've got to be quick. I wanted to let you know a sheriff's deputy came by today."

And there it was. Sean's heartbeat revved right back up.

"We had a fire in town Friday night."

Sean followed his first inclination to play dumb. "Oh, yeah?"

"They think it was arson."

"Really?"

"Yup. Someone saw a car parked at the dead end that night, so the deputy came by to find out whose car it was. I told him it was yours. I reckon the Sheriff's Office will call you, so I'm giving you a heads-up."

"Okay."

"Sorry. I know you didn't have anything to do with that fire, but still, it's a hassle."

"That's alright. Thanks for letting me know."

When Sean hung up, he packed his books in his book bag. He swung it over his shoulder and announced to his roommate he was going to the library.

The roommate gave a distracted okay sign without taking his eyes off the television, and Sean headed down the hallway. As he stepped into the stairwell, he heard the phone ring. *That didn't take long,* he thought, as he bolted down the stairs, two at a time.

The following week was winter quarter finals week. When Sean returned to his dorm room after his first final, his roommate informed him, "That sheriff called again. Third time, now. He's getting testy."

Sean made a conscious effort to show no reaction beyond a nonchalant shrug. "Not sure what he wants, but I need to focus on finals." He placed his bookbag on his desk. "Going to lunch now."

Upon returning from the commons, Sean stepped out of the stairwell into the corridor, and, down the hall, saw his roommate peek out from their opened door. As he turned the corner into his room, Sean heard his roommate say, "Here he is." He held the handset out to Sean with his hand over the mouthpiece. "It's your stalker."

Sean backed out of the doorway and whispered, "Say I'm not here."

"Too late. I already told him you just came back."

Sean groaned silently, clenched his teeth, and took three deep breaths before taking the handset. "Hello?"

"Sean, this is Homer County Sheriff Andy Troyer."

Sean's heart lurched. *It's not just some deputy…it's The Sheriff himself!*

"You're a hard person to get hold of."

"I'm really busy right now." Sean stalled, gulping for air. Somehow, his fluttering heart was interfering with his breathing. It took considerable effort to squeak out a few more words: "It's finals week."

"Uh-huh. Look, I'd like to sit down with you and chat. Do you mind if I come down tomorrow?"

Wait…was Sheriff Andy Troyer prepared to spend the better part of a day just to "chat?" Sean wasn't sure he got that right. "Come down here? To Columbus?"

"Yes."

Sean swallowed. "Like I said, this is finals week."

"Yeah, I heard you. How about Wednesday?"

"I have two finals that day."

"When is your last final?"

Although his last final was Wednesday, Sean said, "Thursday."

"Hmmm." A pen clicked repeatedly from the sheriff's end of the line, then fell silent. He blew out a long breath. "I can't make it down Thursday. Will you be in Homer County on Friday?"

Suddenly, more than ever, Sean wished he were going to the beach for spring break, like his roommate. He squeezed his eyes shut as he considered lying, then cleared his throat. "Yeah."

“Okay then. Why don’t you come in and meet me here Friday afternoon?”

Even though the sheriff said it like a question, Sean knew it wasn’t.

Chapter 14

The Homer County Sheriff's Office sat just outside Clarkton, tucked off the state highway on a nondescript township road. Sean parked the Granada in the small parking area in front of the building, stepped out into the drizzle, and followed the walkway to the front entrance.

Having made it through finals week, Sean should have been feeling relaxed. Instead, he had been so freaked out that he'd tossed his cookies before leaving the house. He was praying he wouldn't do it again here, of all places.

"Good morning," a bleached-blonde, middle-aged, gum-chewing woman said from behind a glass wall. "You must be Sean Davidson."

Sean nodded as he used his bare hands to rake the rain out of his hair, trying not to show his alarm over this woman expecting him.

"Sheriff Troyer will meet you in the interview room." She pushed a button to release the door and waved him in.

Interview room. The sound of it made his gut twist.

After a short walk down the hall, the woman stepped aside, motioning him into a barren room with a metal table at the center. "He'll be with you shortly."

Sean stood in the corner and began cracking his knuckles. Shortly after finishing the full cycle, he heard loud footsteps coming his way.

From the sound of them, Sean guessed it was the sheriff — "Large and in charge," as his mother would have said. When a hefty, bald but mustachioed man entered the room and kicked the door closed behind him, Sean thought, *Check and check.*

The sheriff put two paper cups of coffee on the table. He stuck his hand out to Sean. "Sheriff Andy Troyer."

Sean shook his hand but said nothing.

"I brought you coffee. Cream or sugar?"

"Thanks, but I don't drink coffee." Sean lied, figuring this could be a ploy to collect his fingerprints from the cup. Anyway, his stomach was in no shape for consumption.

"Water? Coke?"

"No, thanks," Sean repeated, increasingly feeling like the sheriff was pressing to get him to take hold of something.

When Sheriff Troyer gestured for Sean to sit, he did, but he made a point of scooting the chair forward to the table without touching it with his hands.

The sheriff plopped down across from him and fished a small spiral notebook from his shirt's front pocket. From the other pocket, he removed a pack of Camels. He tapped one out, then held the pack out for Sean. "Smoke?"

Sean fidgeted with his hands in his lap. "I don't smoke, either."

Andy Troyer shrugged. He reached over to the end of the table and grabbed a cast metal ashtray, fashioned after the Ohio State "Horseshoe" football stadium, crammed full of cigarette butts. "Did you catch many games last season?"

It took Sean a moment to understand the question. It was the ashtray that helped him connect the dots. "No. I sold all my student tickets. Made some money on them."

The sheriff dug a Bic lighter from his pants pocket and lit his cigarette. "I was thinking about catching one of their spring practices—" He seemed to cut himself off. "Anyway, I don't think this coach is the right guy."

Sean had never followed OSU football closely, and so far, attending school there hadn't sparked an interest. So, he didn't have much to offer on the subject. But all of a sudden, he wondered if watching a spring practice session could have been the real motivation behind the sheriff's offer to travel to Columbus.

Something in the back of Sean's mind reminded him he owed a response. "Yeah, he's not too popular."

The sheriff swung his head to the side and blew out a smoke plume. He turned back to Sean and studied him, like weighing whether football was going to be a meaningful topic of discussion here. He removed a pen from his shirt pocket and clicked it. "So, what I'm hoping you can help us with..." He checked his watch and scrawled something in the notebook. "The night you had that campfire behind Bob Wolf's house—"

"Grand-Bob."

Sheriff Troyer arched an eyebrow at Sean. "Scuse me?"

"We call him Grand-Bob."

The sheriff nodded, jotting down something else.

"Anyway, that night, did you see anything unusual?"

Sean thought, *If only you knew,* but he shook his head. "Like what?"

The sheriff took another drag and slowly blew out the smoke. "What were you doing behind Bob—." He checked his notebook. "—Grand-Bob's house?"

"I had a campfire."

"By yourself?"

"Yes."

"Why?"

Sean narrowed his eyes. "It was the anniversary of my best friend's death."

"That would be Karl Wolf?"

"That's right."

Troyer frowned. "Tragic. I'm sorry for your loss." His frown shifted into a pucker. He scratched his pudgy chin with the hand that wasn't holding the cigarette. "But why have a campfire?"

"The night before he died, that's what we did together."

The sheriff took another puff. "And what time were you back there for this campfire?"

Sean was prepared for this question but put on a show of thinking it through. "I got there before seven..." He paused and bobbed his head, staring across the room. "...I left around eleven. Yeah. Right around eleven."

"Where did you go from there?"

"Home."

The sheriff clicked his pen a few times. "Did you drive through Moravian Village? The town itself, I mean."

Sean folded his arms across his chest. "That's the opposite direction from Clarkton."

"I'm well aware of that. Did you?"

"No. I went straight home."

After another drag, Sheriff Troyer asked, "What time did you get home?"

Sean answered that one promptly. "11:30."

"Are you sure?"

"Yes. I remember looking at the clock when I got there."

"Were your parents still up?"

"No, but my mom woke up when I went to my bedroom a few minutes later. She called hello from across the hall."

Sheriff Troyer leaned back in his chair, took a hit from his smoke, and furrowed his brow. "A house burned down that night. Did you see it?"

"No. Where?"

"In Moravian Village, not far from the square. Do you know anything about that?"

"No."

"You sure?"

"I am."

Sheriff Troyer took one last puff, then crushed his smoke in the stadium ashtray. He put the pen down and rubbed his mustache, giving Sean a long, probing stare. "So, you'll be in town all next week, right?"

Sean nodded. "It's spring break."

"I may have some other questions for you."

"Okay."

"In the meantime..." The sheriff reached into his shirt pocket and pulled out a business card. He slid it across the table. "...if you think of anything that might be useful, call me."

After leaving the Sheriff's Office, Sean stopped at the Bretzler IGA supermarket. He loitered near the pay phone at the front of the store and looked around, making sure nobody he knew was nearby.

Pulling the bag of coins out of his pocket, he noticed it was mostly pennies now. *Better make it quick.*

This time, he dialed Heather's number from memory.

"Hello?"

"Yo, it's me."

"Oh, good. I've been dying here. How did it go?"

Sean ran his fingers through his hair with his free hand. "Hard to say. But I'm not wigging out like I was the past week. I'm thinking this guy was more interested in going to campus to watch a football spring practice session than chatting with me."

"Whatchoo talkin' 'bout Willis?"

Sean laughed. "I kid you not. He's a major OSU football fan. He also doesn't seem like the sharpest knife in the drawer."

"That could work against you," Heather pointed out. "On the other hand, I've been thinking. When Thomas carried that can and the Roman candle, it seems like most of your fingerprints would have been lost."

"Yeah, I've thought about that too. The problem is, it only takes one. Anyway, I made a point of not touching anything during my visit."

"You'd better lie low. Don't go near Moravian Village anytime soon."

"I'll stay clear until the thirteenth of June."

"What's going on then?"

"That's the last day of spring quarter."

"And?"

"Remember how I told you I'll be taking that scuba diving class?"

"Of course."

"When school breaks, I'm going diving in that river." Sean pressed his open palm against his forehead and closed his eyes. "As long as I'm not in jail, that is."

Chapter 15

When Sean turned onto the block centered by the Moravi-Yum Donut shop, he immediately spotted Heather's white Chevette parked directly across the street. He pulled the Granada into the open space behind it.

She waved at him through the shop window as he climbed out. Seeing Heather gave Sean the familiar tingle of excitement. It had been a long three months since he'd last laid eyes on her, even though the harrowing events of the eighth of March seemed like yesterday.

The bell clattered when he opened the door, and Big Boy peeked out from the back, grinning as if he recognized Sean.

"Hey there," Heather said, standing to greet him with a hug.

Although Sean was prepared for the embrace this time, he came in from the wrong angle, so it still turned out clumsy.

"And finally, here we are, once again," Heather said as she released him. "Are you ready for this?"

Sean let out a sigh. He started to crack his knuckles, but caught himself. "Yeah. I guess."

Heather shook her head as if to clear it and gestured to the table, where two sandwiches and two cans of pop were waiting. "I already ordered lunch. Roast beast and cheddar, right?"

Sean chuckled as he took his seat. "My fave! *Roast beast*...where is that from?"

She slid Sean's sandwich over to him, along with a can of A&W Root Beer. "The best Christmas show of all time! That's what the Whos eat on the big day."

He slapped his forehead. "How could I forget? When I was a kid, I *lived* for *The Grinch*." He opened his pop and took a sip. "You didn't need to buy."

"You bought the last time, remember? When the shop was about to close?"

"Okay. Well, merci."

"De nada." Heather opened her 7 Up. "How did the quarter end up?"

Sean made a "so-so" rocking hand gesture. "I'll know in two weeks when I get my grades. I passed my scuba test, though."

"Stellar!" Heather held up an open hand, and Sean high-fived her.

"And I found out Monday I landed that summer internship. Starting next week, I'll be doing those environmental survey dives."

Heather held out both hands. "Double high-five!"

Sean responded with a two-handed slap.

"Where is this job based?"

"Columbus. I signed a summer sublet near campus. But I'll be doing fieldwork all over central Ohio."

"I'm going to a writer's conference at OSU in a couple weeks. Maybe I'll see you there."

Sean acted casual, resisting the urge to press for a concrete plan. He made a note to bring it up later, though.

Heather took a swig of her pop. "Still no word from the sheriff?"

"Nope. I'm starting to think I might be in the clear." Sean went to knock on the tabletop, but promptly realized it was metal. Instead, he knocked on the wooden windowsill.

Heather knocked too, then took a bite of her sandwich. Before she had swallowed, she raised a finger and said, "Mmmm..." She pulled a booklet from her purse and placed it on the table. "I got here early, so I stopped by the Moravian Village Historical Museum." She slid the booklet across the table. "I bought this there."

Sean picked it up and read the front cover.

Massacre at Moravian Village
Blackest Page in History of Northwest Territory

"It's about the Indian massacre?"

Heather nodded grimly. "In those days, Ohio was part of the Northwest Territory. The museum has displays about what happened, but I didn't have time to look through them. I'll be reading this, though."

Sean paged through the booklet, promptly recognizing an older writing style in the long paragraphs. It reminded him of the high school literature class he had suffered through.

As if reading his mind, Heather said, "It was written in 1843."

Sean handed her the booklet.

"I also found the burned house." Heather pointed sideways with her thumb. "It backs up to the cemetery. All charred up and boarded over now. It's so sad."

Sean stared out the window, conjuring the image of that burned-out house he'd repeatedly formed in his mind's eye over the past three months. The handiwork of Thomas. This year's killing. *Killings,* he corrected himself. *Plural.* "Five dead now."

Heather frowned. "Six, if you count Jack's overdose. Like collateral damage."

They lapsed into silence as they nibbled on their sandwiches. Eventually, Heather spoke. "So, you're all set with Grand-Bob?"

Sean gave a thumbs-up. After a few more chews, he swallowed. "I told him I wanted to practice scuba diving in the river."

Heather let out a huff. "He must think you're mental."

Sean laughed. "Anybody else would, but not Grand-Bob. He just goes with the flow."

Heather chewed the inside of her cheek and fidgeted with her locket. After a while, she tilted her head and searched Sean's face. "Are you nervous?"

He shrugged. "Maybe a little." He pretended to watch an older couple pass by the window, wondering if he appeared as anxious as he felt. However, he was determined to keep a brave face with Heather, even though he could sense her own angst.

"So, what exactly are you expecting to find down there?"

He held out both hands, palms up. "God knows. With any luck, I'll find out where this freak is going." Sean pressed the tip of his index finger against his temple. "How would we ever stop him if we don't know that?"

Sean stared at the river, trying to see beyond the surface. Small fish flitted along the bank, but the lighter-colored bottom disappeared from view just a few feet from shore, where the water turned deep and murky.

The river had plenty of stretches shallow enough to walk across, but not in this section, where the bend in the waterway had scoured out a deep hole. His thoughts veered back to the memory of his treacherous river crossing. *You were damn lucky,* he thought. Of course, Karl had played a role in his survival...unless that was all just a figment of Sean's near-death brain.

"You couldn't have asked for a nicer day," Heather said.

Sean peeled his gaze away from the river, tilted his head back, and turned his eyes upward at the crystal blue sky. "For sure." But while the air carried the warmth of early summer, the river would still hold a lingering chill, so he'd brought his shorty wetsuit.

Knowing he'd have limited visibility in the river, Sean's search plan was to zigzag across, starting here, opposite from where Heather had hidden inside the evergreen, to an equal distance downstream from the park bench near the cemetery entrance. If he couldn't find anything within that span, he'd need to refill his tanks and return another day for a wider sweep.

"Ready or not, here I come," he announced, stepping over to the pile of gear they'd deposited on the bank.

Heather sat on a fallen log and pulled out the booklet she'd picked up at the Historical Society. She watched Sean wiggle the wetsuit over his swimsuit and slip his arms into the tank backpack, grunting under the weight. Next came the face mask, which he tightened and adjusted to ensure a good fit. He then wrapped the weight belt around his waist and attached the dive knife.

"That's your protection?"

"Divers carry knives in case they get tangled up in something. But yeah, it might come in handy for self-defense, too."

"Probably better than a Roman candle." Heather gave a teasing smile.

Sean laughed, welcoming the diversion of humor. "Especially underwater."

Heather joined him in laughter, but tapered off abruptly. "I guess we shouldn't joke about it, considering what Thomas did with your Roman candle."

He nodded and straightened his face. After a somber moment, he scooted down to the water's edge and began slipping his feet into the fins.

She watched him silently, then said, "I wish I knew how to scuba dive."

Sean was unsure whether she meant she'd like to help or was simply down for the adventure of it all. He debated whether to confess how wigged out he felt about the "adventure" he was about to embark on. But since the whole thing had been his idea in the first place, he let it go.

When he stepped into the river, cold water sent a chilling sensation up Sean's legs. He gritted his teeth, stood upright, and said, "With any luck, I'll find my shoes."

Heather snorted. "Unless Thomas ran off with them."

"Good point. He could use a new pair."

Heather laughed even harder, but their shared nervous mood dampened it quickly.

Grabbing the yellow dive lamp, he switched it on, throwing a bright circle of light onto the bank. He wrapped his lips around the mouthpiece and opened the valve. After drawing a breath, he stepped backward into the river, dropped waist-deep, and clenched his jaw against the coldness shocking his lower body.

Sean steeled himself, leaned back, and dropped into the water. He raised his hand in what he hoped looked like a courageous wave.

Heather returned his wave, but the last thing he saw before he dove below the surface was the worry on her face, which didn't help.

The silent underwater world enveloped him as he rolled over and gave a few kicks to move into deeper water. He held up there to take it all in. His nerves tightened as he surveilled the environment for movement. Sunlight illuminated the upper layer of the water, but suspended silt darkened the water below.

Sean kicked his fins, propelling himself toward the middle. He aimed downward and made a few more strokes to descend.

For a moment, he saw nothing, but when the dive light's beam fell on something reaching up from the obscured depths, his heart seized. The thunder inside his chest ebbed a bit with the realization it was merely the roots of a submerged tree trunk. He hovered over it, carving through the darkness of cloudy water with the dive light.

A traffic cone lay discarded on the river floor, the orange color barely visible under a coating of silt. Various bottles and cans lay scattered in the vicinity, amongst the natural debris of rocks and sunken tree limbs. A good-sized smallmouth bass swam toward Sean, regarded him for a moment, then darted away.

A tire, half embedded in the muck, was the next thing Sean spotted, just before the river bottom began sloping up toward the opposing bank. Sean held up there, monitoring his surroundings while he floated downstream with the current, before doubling back.

As the minutes passed without any sign of Thomas, the tension began draining from Sean's body, aided by the relaxing sensation of gliding underwater. He now saw firsthand how river diving was a much different experience than diving in the stone quarry where he'd trained. That body of water lacked moving currents, wasn't clouded with silt, and its floor was devoid of foreign objects. Aside from the risk of Thomas's presence, this was *far* more interesting.

Sean drifted above a discarded wheelbarrow, then the river bottom began sloping upward, toward the bank where Heather waited. A school of spotfin shiner fish parted as he kicked toward the surface.

When he emerged, Heather looked up from her reading with a startled expression. Sean had come up twenty feet downriver from where he'd started. They exchanged waves before he dove back down, turning back for his next diagonal lap.

A sudden movement caught Sean's eye as he swept over a knot of submerged trees. He flinched, then realized it was a grouping of darter fish, now receding into the tendrils of a tree's roots. He pushed on, and when he reached the opposite bank once again, he pivoted around and headed back to Heather's side.

A folded-up lawn chair sticking out from the muddy bottom prompted Sean to wonder how so much junk ended up in the river. Was it intentionally thrown there? Or was it the result of occasional floods?

When he arrived at the upward slope, he popped out of the water. Heather, who had moved downstream several paces, was expecting him this time. After a quick wave, she went back to her reading. Sean dove down and kicked across, passing over another tire along the way.

As he approached the opposite side, he prepared to make his turn, but hesitated. A section of chain-link fencing was wedged over a dimple on the rising bank. The dark indentation in the slope was barely noticeable, hidden behind the tangled scrap of fence.

Sean drew in, steering the light into a gap between the wires, illuminating what appeared to be a hollow. He braced himself with his knees against the slope. A solid tug on the chain-link freed it from the muddy bank. As the fencing fell away, Sean examined the exposed open tunnel. Wide enough for him to comfortably enter, the passage extended beyond the reach of his light.

His first thought was that this was a culvert—a drainage pipe feeding into the river. But when he looked more carefully, he could see the opening wasn't lined in concrete. The walls were clay, the surface carved in uneven gouges.

Was there any chance an animal could have done this? Sean wanted to tell himself it was possible, but there was no way. It was far too big to be a mink or a muskrat den. *Maybe a beaver?* Sure, beavers were tunnel diggers, but underneath their dams, rather than a random spot like this. And then, there's that chain-link fence. No animal would have wedged that in.

Sean pushed his torso into the hollow, extending his arm to shine the light as far as possible. But the shaft continued on some distance further.

He considered whether he should venture in. His scuba certification was for open-water diving only. Diving in enclosed spaces like caves and shipwrecks carried unique dangers and required specialized training, none of which Sean had.

But still... He examined the tunnel walls, using his arms to gauge the width. They weren't particularly narrow, so he could turn around in this space if he had to. He grabbed a handful of the clay lining, which tore off easily. There was nothing he could snag on. *How dangerous could it be?* The diving risk, that is.

Sean wrestled with his thoughts. Part of him wanted to turn back. Another part of him said he *must* investigate. Maybe this was nothing; if so, he needed to rule it out. *Just ten feet,* he told himself. A compromise. That would take him further than the limited reach of his beam, maybe far enough to catch a glimpse of what lay beyond.

Sean would not have gone down that tunnel if he had thought about it long enough. So, he decided to quit thinking about it. *To hell with caution,* he thought. *That's what Karl would say.* He propelled himself into the hole with a swift kick of his fins.

The darkness swallowed him, but with no currents to stir up the sediment, the further he went down the length of the passage, the clearer the water became. The light beam still fell on nothing, though. Just more tunnel.

Something jarred Sean's body, and it took him a second to realize his tank had scraped against the top of the passage. A cloud of sediment blossomed all around him. While the hole wasn't particularly narrow, he had to be careful to stay in the center. He used his free hand to steer himself along the tunnel's bottom, which helped him maintain his position.

As he proceeded down the passageway, a claustrophobic feeling took hold. *Don't go there,* he pleaded with himself, fighting off the feeling that the tunnel walls were closing in on him. He even stopped to re-gauge the width by pressing his hands on either side, judging no change in the angle of his arms. *See? The walls are* not *closing in.*

But then another thought crept into his mind: *What if the tunnel collapses?* A choking sensation took hold of him, and suddenly, his wetsuit felt too tight on his torso. *Keep it together,* he commanded, fighting to clear the paranoid thoughts.

Had he gone ten feet yet? Looking back would only slow him down, so he had to guess. But just when he decided he must have gone at least that far, he noticed the tunnel appeared to be sloping upward. A few feet further, the change was evident.

The cautious part of Sean's brain warned him, *You've already gone too far*. But another part of his brain overruled the idea of turning back. He paddled his fins and wafted ahead.

Once he had penetrated the upward-sloping segment, he trained the light forward. The beam glinted in a distant reflection. This was the underside of the water's surface, which meant the tunnel extended above the water level. Where did it go from there?

Although his heart was galloping in his chest, he imagined Karl saying, *There's only one way to find out.*

Without allowing himself the opportunity to second-guess his decision, Sean gave a swift kick and propelled toward the reflection.

Chapter 16

SEAN SLOWED AS HE drew near the surface, wary of what might lie beyond. He inched forward the last few feet, bracing himself as his facemask punched through the reflective glimmer.

Nothing was waiting for him on the other side, though. The tunnel continued at the same upward angle for a body length, then tilted back to a flat pitch.

Sean bobbed on the water's surface, questioning whether he should proceed. If he did, there was no telling what he faced, and movement outside the water would be slower, making escape more difficult.

You can't turn back now, he told himself, thinking of Karl and Heather's mother. Without another thought, he began army-crawling up the clay incline.

The tank grew heavier on his back as he emerged from the water, but he kept his mask and air supply on, figuring there would be little or no oxygen underground. The tight clay walls hushed the sound of his labored breathing as though he were locked inside a crypt.

When his head cleared the change in pitch, he paused to scan the extended visual field with the light and discovered that the tunnel widened another body length ahead. He pushed himself onward, straining for a better view.

As he approached the widening, Sean gasped. The tunnel opened into a subterranean chamber smaller than his bedroom, with a crudely carved domed ceiling too low to stand under. He pulled into the clearing and shimmied onto his knees, sitting on his heels with his free palm on the floor.

Sean studied the ceiling, the dive torch trembling in his grip. Light gray protrusions jutted from its surface, increasing in density near the dome's apex. Sean squinted, trying to work out what the protrusions were. Then it clicked.

Bones. Dozens of them. No, hundreds.

He squeezed his eyes closed in revulsion, but fought the urge to flee. *What is this?*

Seconds later, he went rigid as he answered his own question.

I'm underneath the massacre burial site!

Thinking back on the orientation and length of the tunnel, it all made horrible sense.

Survival instinct took over, and he found himself turning back in the direction from which he'd come. But then he thought better of it and forced himself to hold his ground. Did any other shafts radiate out from the underground alcove? When he swept the light across the chamber's perimeter, he found none, but something nestled in a depression at the center caught his eye.

Sean rose on his knees, leaned forward, and trained the light on it for a better look. What he saw struck him hard. He recoiled and blinked, but there was no denying the hideous sight.

Thomas's withered body lay lodged in a trench on the floor.

Sean swallowed what felt like a glob of clay. He stared at the ghastly figure, feeling a wave of goosebumps run down his back. Fully expecting Thomas to rise and lunge at him, Sean tensed his muscles, preparing to lurch away at the slightest hint of movement.

But Thomas lay motionless, facing away, revealing the grotesque head wound Sean had first glimpsed by the campfire. Heavy fabric clothing, filthy and torn, covered much of his shriveled body, with gray, leathery skin clinging to the exposed parts of his limbs.

Sean shifted his eyes down to Thomas's feet. The leather foot coverings, attached with thongs, cinched tight, tied in knots, had been blackened with fire.

Seconds ticked away, stacking into a full minute, but still, there was no sign of motion. Although Sean was not about to go near the body, by all accounts, Thomas appeared lifeless.

Except Thomas could not be *entirely* lifeless. No doubt some tiny ember of energy still smoldered somewhere deep within that wasted body, and on the eighth of March, Thomas would rise again.

As Sean's initial panic subsided, he allowed his gaze to stray past Thomas. Several items had been arranged on the opposite side of the trench. "Hey," Sean said out loud into the mouthpiece, holding his voice below a whisper. "That's Karl's lighter!" Despite the Winston logo being obscured by smears of clay, the unique shape gave it away. He resisted the urge to retrieve it and examined the other items: an ancient knife, a leather pouch, a large wooden mallet, and a shovel.

Sean remembered the leather pouch from the campfire and figured the shovel likely belonged to Marcus. He was considering whether Thomas might have used the large wooden mallet to club Jack and Marcus when he felt a sharp pain on the crown of his head.

Ducking lower, Sean put his hand there and felt something slimy in his hair. He pulled at it, only to discover it was attached to his scalp. *What in God's name?* His mind exploded in terror. He snatched at the thing and squeezed it, tearing it off his head. When he opened his hand in front of his mask, he found the remnants of...an *earthworm?*

He flung it away and looked up. Had his head brushed against the ceiling? Yeah, most likely. But what the hell was that?

Sean pointed the light beam at the ceiling and stared at it. The surface seemed to be moving, no, *writhing*. With his diving mask obscuring his view, he pushed it onto his forehead for a better look, and that's when he saw countless earthworms protruding from the clay above, each wiggling in the air for a few seconds before retreating.

Stifling a scream, Sean whirled around, yanked the mask back down over his eyes, and clambered back into the tunnel.

Sean shot out of the river like a whale breaching the ocean, causing Heather to jump in shock. He attempted to scamper up the muddy slope, but tripped on his fins, crashing into the bank instead.

"Are you okay?" Heather asked as she hurried over to help.

Sean expected her to laugh at his clumsiness, but she didn't. He tore the facemask off, spat out the mouthpiece, and squirmed the tank off his back. "Oh, my God! I found Thomas!"

Heather's eyes grew large.

Panting, Sean pointed across the river. "There's a tunnel." He gulped in a breath. "On that side. It ends under the burial mound. That's where he goes."

Heather looked across the river, squinting, like trying to see through the ground. "You went in it?"

"Yeah." Sean shivered, yanked off his fins, and brushed the debris off himself.

"What did he do?"

"Nothing. He never moved. It's like he's...hibernating, or something. He's all dried out. Just lying in wait."

"Until the eighth of March rolls around," Heather added, gazing across the river.

"You pegged it." Sean touched the tender spot on his head and tried not to wince.

Still looking away, Heather pressed an open palm against her cheek and furrowed her brow. "That's so warped."

Sean discreetly checked his fingertip and found a spot of blood. He grimaced at the sight but held off on telling Heather about the flesh-eating worms. *Save that one for later.*

He pushed himself onto his feet, which seemed to draw Heather back into herself. She held up the booklet she'd been reading. "Well, you won't believe what I learned."

Sean noticed then that her eyes were red and swollen. She'd been crying. "Fill me in. Take your time."

Heather took a long look at the cover and drew a deep breath. "The Indians lived here in a Christian Moravian missionary settlement. They stayed out of the Revolutionary War, but a Pennsylvania militia group raided their village. The men accused these people of attacking Americans and spying for the British. They sentenced them to death."

Heather fell silent for a moment. She blinked and sniffed, then continued, her eyes still fixed on the booklet. "They bludgeoned them with a wooden mallet, then scalped them. Yeah, white people scalped the natives."

Sean felt a wave of lightheadedness. He leaned against a nearby tree trunk to steady himself.

"Almost one hundred innocent people were massacred, mostly women and children." Heather's voice sounded strangled. "They threw the corpses into the log buildings and burned them."

She turned away and stared at something off in the distance, as if working to collect her emotions. After a long pause, she resumed. "Only one lived to tell what happened. A thirteen-year-old boy somehow survived the blow to his head and the scalping."

Sean pressed his palm against his forehead, trying to imagine how anyone could survive being scalped.

"The boy ran off to warn others at a nearby settlement so they could escape the same fate. He was a hero, but his days were numbered."

Heather turned back to Sean with dark eyes and a tight face. "He suffered from convulsions because of his head injuries, and before long, he had a seizure while crossing a river. He drowned, but they never found his body."

Heather's eyes hung on Sean's as she let that sink in. "Guess his name."

Sean felt what he would have sworn was a tarantula crawling up the back of his neck. "Whoa. No way."

A fresh tear rolled down Heather's cheek as she nodded grimly. "His name was Thomas."

Heading back, they were halfway across the farm field before either could discuss what they'd discovered. Heather spoke first. "We need to let this go, Sean."

Sean gave her a sidelong glance. She looked as frazzled as he felt. He didn't respond, though. It was like he'd just awakened from a nightmare, and rational thought was still out of reach.

"We're in over our heads," she added.

Sean stopped to shift his scuba gear bag to his other arm, then resumed the trek along the crop row.

Were they in over their heads? Probably. But could they just walk away? How could they?

"Tell me what you're thinking," she prompted after a long stretch of silence.

Sean puffed out his cheeks and blew out slowly. "I don't know. I need time to come to grips with all this."

Heather gave one of those disbelieving headshakes. "It's so mind-blowing."

He swallowed. "Mind-blowing is right. I'm not sure what I expected, but finding him made this whole thing so much more...real."

"Most definitely. And knowing Thomas is tied to that massacre over two hundred years ago...it feels...I don't know...*bigger* now."

Sean blinked repeatedly, his unseeing gaze centered on the Granada parked at the dead end beyond the field.

"What are we dealing with here?" Heather asked.

"Good question," Sean said. "A *corpse* comes to life once a year. No biologist would ever say that's possible."

"What would the police do?"

Sean stiffened. "We *can't* go to the police. The sheriff probably still considers me a person of interest for that fire."

After a dozen silent paces, Heather asked, "What about a priest?"

Sean considered this. "I don't know. Are we talking about an exorcism?"

She narrowed her eyes. "Maybe not. I mean, it's not like Thomas is a living person who's possessed." She paused, then cleared her throat. "Aren't there paranormal investigators out there?"

"Yeah, but...I always thought those people were quacks."

Heather gave a sober chuckle. "Isn't that what people would call *us*?"

He shrugged. She was right, though. Anyhow, where would they even find these quacks? They weren't going to be in the Yellow Pages.

"So, what do we do now?" she asked.

Sean had no answer. But if Heather pulled out, wouldn't he also have to? He could *not* let her make that decision. Not yet, at least. "We need time to digest this. We can't decide anything right now."

Her mouth opened as if she was going to say something, but then she closed it and pursed her lips.

By the time they reached the end of the field, Heather finally responded. "You're right. We need time. I'll be in Columbus for that writer's conference in two weeks. Let's meet there, and then we'll decide what to do."

Chapter 17

The room Sean had sublet for the summer was student housing at its worst. The ad had referred to it as a "studio apartment," but Sean immediately recognized it was living space converted from the old home's attic.

What he had failed to anticipate was how hot that attic-turned-studio would get during the summer months. In the first week, he figured out that if he turned the AC off, the apartment would take several hours to cool down to a tolerable temperature once he turned it back on. So, although it was only eight in the morning, he would keep the room's sole window unit running.

Before leaving, Sean took another look at the new zit on his cheek, hoping to convince himself it wasn't so bad. It was, though. *Great timing,* he thought, shaking his head at his misfortune. A few months shy of twenty, he wondered how old he'd be when he finally stopped breaking out.

He suddenly realized he hadn't allowed much time. Not wanting to keep Heather waiting, he took the long fire escape stairway two steps at a time and set off on a light jog toward High Street. The peak summer heat had him sweating halfway there, but he kept up the pace.

Sure enough, when Buckeye Donuts came into view, so did Heather, jogging from campus toward High Street, wearing a neon pink and electric blue running outfit and a bright yellow headband across her forehead. She waved and stopped for the walk signal.

Sean waited in front of the doughnut shop, trying to ready himself for the greeting hug. It came when Heather hopped up the curb. This time, he felt he managed it without dorking out too badly. He would have been self-conscious about the sweat he'd worked up, but Heather had him beat in that department. He didn't mind.

Sean pulled the door open and stepped aside. He noticed a pimple on Heather's cheek, too, which goosed up his confidence a tad. "How's the writer's conference going?"

"Eh." Heather scrunched her nose as she led the way into the shop. "Writers are weird." She chuckled, although the way she did it made it seem like she wasn't joking.

"Your mom seemed normal."

Heather reflexively reached for her locket and twiddled it between her fingers. She'd even worn it during her run. "Yeah, sort of. But she would have stuck out in *that* crowd."

She stopped and made a show of looking around. "Hey, how come we always meet in doughnut shops?"

Sean laughed. "They're the only places that sell apple fritters, that's why."

"Good point." Heather rubbed her tummy in the "yum" gesture. "You've got me hooked."

They placed their orders, and Sean carried a tray with their doughnuts and coffees to the window-side counter.

"Oh, this place is decked out in the school colors," Heather said, as if she had just made the connection.

"Yup. Cop a squat on that scarlet stool at this gray counter."

Once settled, Heather picked up her coffee and took a sip. "How's the summer internship?"

Sean had already taken a bite of his apple fritter. He washed it down with a swig of coffee. "It sucks, so far. No diving yet. I spent yesterday pulling invasive weeds. That was fun...not! But we're supposed to do a river survey next week if the weather cooperates."

"I'll keep my fingers crossed for you."

An awkward silence fell between them. With the idle talk having run its course, the elephant in the room grew larger. Sean hesitated to broach the topic of Thomas, though, fearing Heather would tell him she was pulling out. What would he do then?

"I took a detour on the way down," she said, dabbing sweat from her face with a napkin.

"Oh, yeah?"

Heather nodded and fixed her gaze on her coffee cup. "I stopped in Moravian Village."

There it was. Sean turned to her and studied her expression. Did this mean she was still in?

She picked up her cup and took a sip. "I spent over two hours at the museum."

Sean forced himself to nibble on his doughnut, allowing her time to continue at her own pace.

"Most of their displays talk about the massacre. The more I learn about it, the sicker I feel."

He nodded somberly. "Were the men who did it ever punished?"

Heather sighed. "Not a one." She stared out the window, but her eyes didn't seem to focus on anything in particular.

After a while, she sniffed, then took another drink of coffee. "Thomas is mentioned in one of the museum displays." She turned to face Sean. "I'm still trying to get my head around you finding him down there."

Sean wiped both hands down his face, like trying to scrub away the disturbing memory. "Tell me about it."

"When I think about who Thomas is..." Heather gave a quick shake of her head. "...who he was..." She rubbed her lips with her fingers. "I can't help but feel sorry for him."

Sean snapped his head toward her. "*Sorry* for him?"

"Yeah, I know. Totally mental, right? He killed my mom, and now I'm feeling bad for him?"

Sean began cracking his knuckles. Where was she going with this? Was she angling to let Thomas off the hook?

"At first, I thought of Thomas as just a cold-blooded killer. But now, I keep thinking about what he went through." Heather shifted on the stool as she gathered her words. "He watched his people get murdered. He somehow survived his own injuries and ran off to warn others. Think about the trauma he went through."

"He killed Karl." The words tumbled out of Sean's mouth without conscious thought. "He killed your mom."

Heather chewed on her lower lip. "True. But think about it..." She tapped a finger on her temple. "His body was lying there—harmlessly—for *two hundred years*. It wasn't until some idiot desecrated the grave of his people that Thomas started killing."

"So?"

"So, maybe he was just protecting the burial site. If a hornet stings you after you kick its nest, you can't exactly blame the hornet."

"Alright, so he was protecting the burial site. But he didn't stop there, did he?"

Heather frowned. "Look, I'm not taking Thomas's side here. But when I step back and think about everything from his perspective, I can find a sliver of sympathy for him."

Feeling his stomach clench, Sean turned and faced the window. They had talked about avenging Karl and Marilyn's deaths. Now, it seemed like Heather was abandoning him on that quest. Was this how she'd justify pulling out?

A little voice in Sean's head ordered, *Calm down and listen to what she's saying.* He picked up his coffee cup and took a gulp. As much as he hated Thomas for what Thomas had done to Karl, he had to admit there was some sense in her words. How did Thomas feel about what had been done to his people?

Sean blew out an audible breath and turned back to Heather. "I can see your point if I think about it that way. But still, we need to stop him."

"No duh. I'm not saying we should leave him be."

Sean noted to himself how she had said, "We." *That sounds promising.*

"Of course, we need to stop him," she continued. "But *how?*"

"I have a plan."

Heather cocked an eyebrow. "Oh, you do, do you? Does it involve fire?"

Sean froze, scrambling for some way to answer while hanging onto his dignity.

She scoffed. "How did that work out the last time?"

He folded his arms across his chest. "Well..."

Heather rolled her eyes. "Let me guess. You're thinking *more* firepower, right?"

He frowned sheepishly.

"Pfft. Here's the problem, Sean. If he's already dead, he can't be destroyed."

Unable to look her in the eye, Sean turned on his stool and stared out the window again, at a loss for words.

"I trusted you last time," Heather said. "Look where that got us. This time, you need to listen to *me.*"

Sean knew he was in no position to argue, so he remained quiet. Besides, if it meant she was still with him, so be it.

"Believe me, I understand the appeal of payback. But we need to put vengeance aside."

He scratched his chin and turned back to face Heather.

"Thomas will only stop if he lets it all go. If we could go back in time and punish the monsters who massacred those innocent people, that would make a difference." She shook her head. "But justice was never served, and nobody can fix that now. Our only chance is to find a way to help Thomas forgive and forget. If we can do that, he'll rest in peace."

Heather's words echoed in Sean's head. *Forgive and forget. Rest in peace.* There was wisdom in what she said. *We need to put vengeance aside.* Revenge was driving Thomas. Was revenge driving Sean? His shoulders slumped. "Okay, so, what exactly are you suggesting?"

She raised her hands, palms up. "I have no clue. See, that's my point. We need help."

Sean narrowed his eyes. "But from who?"

Heather tapped her fingers on the countertop. "I'm thinking of Thomas's descendants."

With a scrunched face, Sean asked, "His descendants?"

"When I visited the museum, I learned the massacred Indians were part of three Moravian Christian missionary settlements in that area. Some of the fifty survivors, whom Thomas had warned, resettled in Canada after escaping. Their descendants still live in that area on a First Nations reserve."

Heather pointed north. "Southern Ontario, straight across Lake Erie from Ohio."

"So, you're going to try to contact them?"

Heather pulled out a folded piece of paper and opened it, revealing her handwriting. "I'm drafting a letter to the chief."

Sean formed an O with his mouth.

"I don't know, Sean. Maybe these people will think I'm a nutcase. But if there's anyone who might not think this whole thing is insane, it's *got* to be them."

Sean checked his mailbox when he got home from work, as he did every day. Usually, it was junk mail addressed to "Current Resident." Some of it was addressed to the student he was subletting from, which he would toss in a box on the kitchen floor.

On this day, he found an envelope addressed to "Sean Davidson," with "H. Warner" written in the corner, above a Fairlawn, Ohio, address. Standing beside his mailbox, Sean immediately ripped the envelope open.

August 1, 1985

Dear Sean,

I'm so psyched to give you this update. I sent that letter to the chief and explained the whole story. I half expected he'd think I was crazy and never respond, but he gave my letter to a woman in his community named Tessa.

Tessa wrote back right away. She knew all about the massacre and the story of Thomas, having grown up hearing about it from her community's elders.

Tessa has the ability to communicate with spirits. Growing up, she was afraid of this gift but accepted it in recent years, which made it stronger. Her grandma also has this ability and has been teaching Tessa to use it. Because Tessa has this gift, she said she thought she could help and would call me to discuss it.

I just hung up after our call, and we worked out a plan. We will need your help. It's too much to explain here, but in a nutshell: Tessa will drive down from Canada in late September and bring her grandparents. They'll pick me up at Kent State on the way, and we'll meet you in Moravian Village. Hopefully, you've been getting a lot of scuba diving practice in your internship, because you're going to need it!

Please call me Sunday night, and I'll share more.

Catch you later, alligator!
Heather

Chapter 18

Sean pressed the Stop button on his Walkman as he drove across the bridge into Moravian Village. The music's calming distraction had kept him from wigging out.

After taking Music Appreciation during his freshman year, Sean became a big fan of classical music. Beethoven was one of his favorites. He bought cassette tapes for each of the nine Beethoven symphonies and kept rotating through them. During the first hour of the drive, he listened to Symphony No. 6, followed by Symphony No. 7, which he ran out of time to finish. At least he caught the second movement—the best part, by far.

Of course, the downside to listening to classical music while driving was the road noise, which could drown out the quiet parts. Particularly in a beater like the Granada, and especially in the past week since his muffler patch had rusted away.

Road noise wasn't a problem with rock, which was *always* loud. Sean still loved rock, so he alternated between the two. The drive back to Columbus would be late, so hard rock would be on the playlist. Maybe AC/DC...for Karl. *That* would help keep Sean awake.

Sean checked his hair in the rearview mirror as he turned onto the library's street. It was just before two o'clock, their designated meeting time. He scanned the area but saw no sign of Heather with the others.

He parked the Granada along the curb, across the street from the library, and killed the engine. Six months prior, this was where Heather had parked, to let Sean warm up after his ill-fated attempt at cremating Thomas. Sean cringed, thinking about how unprepared he'd been that night. Here he was, once again. Would this attempt have a better outcome?

Remaining in his car, Sean cracked his knuckles as he thought through what lay ahead. The plan had been defined since mid-summer. Now, on the verge of autumn, the day had finally arrived.

A station wagon came his way. Could that be them? No. It was an old, blue-haired woman with a poodle sitting on her lap. Next came a pickup truck, which he immediately ruled out. Four people wouldn't fit in that.

At 2:15, after three other false alarm vehicles had come through, a yellow and white Volkswagen Bus came rumbling his way from the opposite direction. Sean eyed the license plate. It had the same blue-on-white color scheme as Ohio's plates, except the blue lettering appeared darker. Sure enough, as the vehicle approached, he read ONTARIO, written along the top.

Sitting in the front passenger seat, Heather pointed at Sean and waved. Sean took the driver to be Tessa, and he presumed the older couple occupying the back seat were her grandparents.

As the Volkswagen parked against the sandstone curb, directly in front of the library, Sean hopped out and crossed the street. Heather was the first to exit the Bus, and they met in front of the vehicle. "Hey," she said, opening her arms for a hug.

"Hey." This time, Sean executed the hug like a pro. When they pulled apart, he said, "I almost didn't recognize you without your white Chevette."

Heather pretended to smack him.

"Check it out." Sean pointed at the Ohio State "Block O" logo on her sweatshirt, which had the word BUCKEYES embroidered above it. "You're wearing my school's logo."

"*Our* school's logo."

Sean raised his eyebrows. "Huh?"

"I'm transferring in, starting winter quarter."

Sean thought, *Damn, after only a couple of weeks at Kent State?* But he kept that to himself and delivered a blank stare instead.

While Tessa climbed out from behind the wheel, he asked, "What's your boyfriend say about that?"

Heather gave a dismissive wave. "That didn't work out."

Tessa circled the front end of the Volkswagen, cutting off the conversation. Heather said, "Tessa, meet Sean."

He tore his gape away from Heather and introduced himself.

"Nice to meet you," Tessa said as they shook hands.

Sean guessed Tessa was in her mid-twenties. She was tall and thin with strong, angular facial features and long, dark hair. A small bear's claw tattoo adorned the side of her eye.

"And here come my grandparents, Norman and Mildred. They'll wait for us this afternoon at the library."

Norman helped Mildred down the step. Sean figured they had to be approaching 80. They had long, gray hair, braided on both sides. Mildred wore a full-length sky-blue skirt, while Norman wore a gray shirt with a colorful pattern covering the front. As they wandered over in an elderly gait, Heather stepped aside, opening the huddle for them.

After introductions and small-talking about the drive down, Tessa turned to Sean. "Are you ready for this?"

Sean chewed his lip. "I think so. We need to get this bastard." He immediately regretted his choice of words but couldn't call them back.

Tessa exchanged glances with Mildred, then turned to Sean with a harsh expression on her face. "I understand your anger, but this isn't about conquering Thomas."

"Sorry," Sean said, raising his hands in surrender. *Don't screw this up, dumbass. We need their help.* He left it at that, figuring the less he said, the better.

A long, awkward moment followed until Heather spurred the conversation forward. "I learned a lot on the drive down," she said to Sean. "Mildred and Tessa have sensed spirits at the massacre site in the past."

Both women nodded in unison.

"There are many spirits there," Tessa said.

Mildred straightened and said to Sean, "I've visited the site seven or eight times through my years. Each time I have sensed spirits."

Eager to hear what these women had to say, Sean pressed his fist against his mouth.

"But Thomas is different," Tessa said.

"Usually, spirits are a metaphysical presence." Mildred pursed her lips and lowered her head, like working out the best way to explain. "They're incorporeal."

"Not Thomas, though," Tessa said. "His spirit is still embodied in what's left of his physical presence."

"*Part* of his spirit, that is," Mildred clarified. "You see, all humans are a mix of good and bad. We believe when Thomas died, the good departed. The bad stayed behind, clinging to his corpse."

Against his better judgment, Sean felt the need to respond. "This is a bad spirit, for sure. He killed my best friend. Heather's mom, too. And others. All innocent."

Mildred sighed. "Heartbreaking, I know. I'm sorry for your loss." She faced Heather. "Both of you." She turned back to Sean. "But remember, Thomas was an innocent victim, too. As were his people."

Norman shifted his stance. With his gaze fixed on the asphalt, he was clearly staying out of this. Like this was his wife's and granddaughter's realm. *They* were the ones who understood such things, Sean imagined him thinking. *They* were the ones with "the gift."

Tessa raised her finger to emphasize the point she was about to make. "Think about how extraordinary Thomas's story is. He should've died in the same brutal way as the others, but he somehow escaped death."

"Yes, it's incredible," Mildred said. "But because of his head injuries, he suffered from convulsions. While crossing the river, he had a seizure. He was believed to have drowned."

"Except, even then, he didn't die *completely*," Tessa said. "What was left of him—the bad part, that is—burrowed underneath his people's graves."

"To be near them," Heather said, as if she too was finally sorting out the puzzle. She turned to Sean. "It's pitiful."

Mildred nodded. "As it turned out, the environment in that chamber preserved his cadaver. Natural mummification, it's called. So, he dwelt there for over two hundred years. Lost to the world. Innocuous."

"That is until some boy desecrated the burial place," Tessa said.

Mildred jumped right back in, taking back the narrative. "This vile act stirred up a protective impulse in Thomas and fueled his thirst for revenge."

Indiscriminate revenge, Sean thought to himself, gritting his teeth. "Two wrongs don't make a right."

"No, they don't," Mildred said. "But instead of simply hating Thomas, we must work to understand him. We must strive for empathy. Only then will we have the chance to reunify his spirit."

"And help him move on," Tessa added.

It occurred to Sean that these women were saying something similar to what Heather had said. *Understanding. Empathy.* He turned the words over, unsure if he had it in him to feel this way about the entity that had killed his best friend. And if so, would he be letting Karl down by embracing this mindset?

After a long pause to allow their words to sink in, Mildred cleared her throat. "Through understanding and empathy, we can prepare Thomas for his final journey from the physical world to the spiritual realm."

"Bringing Thomas peace in eternal rest will break this cycle of revenge," Tessa said.

Another stretch of silence followed before Mildred spoke again. "We must act before the eighth of March. But we can't wait." She tilted her head back and looked at the tree branches above, tinged with fall color. "The seasons are turning, and autumn is setting in. We need the leaf cover to avoid being seen. The time is now; before the leaves fall."

Sean's mouth went dry at the thought of what lay ahead.

"We can't do this alone, Sean." Tessa stepped forward and locked eyes with him. "We need your help. So, I will ask again: Are you ready for this?"

Feeling the eyes of the others on him as well, Sean set his jaw and squared his shoulders. "I'm ready."

Tessa's face softened. "Good. Now let's go over our plan."

Sean felt jittery as he donned his diving gear on the riverbank behind Grand-Bob's house. Heather and Tessa watched him in nervous silence, as if they shared his angst. Except it was he who faced the most dreadful part of the first task.

With his shorty wetsuit zipped up and his tanks and weight belt mounted, Sean sat on the slope and stretched his fins over his feet before dropping them into the river. He attached the diving knife and the stake to one side of his belt, and the rescue harness he'd recently picked up from the dive shop to the other. When his mask was in place and the air supply valve opened, he pushed upright and used his free hand to give a thumbs-up sign to Heather and Tessa.

Heather responded with a quick wave and an uneasy look before picking up the end of the long coil of rope near her feet. Tessa gave Sean two enthusiastic thumbs-ups and took a position on the opposite flank of the coil. Her grandparents had stayed at the library since the trek across the field would have been too much for them, and they weren't needed until nighttime, anyway.

Without letting himself linger, Sean grabbed the carabiner attached to the free end of the rope and slipped into the river. He clenched his jaw against the chilly water, now cooler than that early summer day when he had found Thomas. This time of year, a full-body wetsuit might have been called for, but since Sean didn't feel he could afford one, he'd have to make do.

He plunged into the river, stiffened against the shock of coldness, and extended the lamp forward with one shaky arm. Following the light beam, he propelled himself across, avoiding the depths where the temperature might be even colder.

With his other hand gripping the carabiner, he towed the free end of the rope through the water. When the slope of the opposite bank rose in front of him, he looked it over but found no sign of the tunnel. He used the stake to carve an X in the clay, marking his starting point.

Allowing the current to carry him downriver, he scanned the surface with the light, searching for the tunnel. As the seconds ticked by, Sean began to worry. *What if I don't find it? What then?* He told himself to be patient and continued eyeing the muddy incline while drifting downstream.

Nothing.

Maybe I started too far downriver. Sean gave one last look, then turned back and headed upstream. The rope, pulled by the current, resisted his movement, slowing his pace. He labored against the water's flow and the line's drag, slogging his way past the X.

Not far from where he'd started, Sean caught sight of the section of chain-link fencing he had pulled out from the hole on his last drive, resting on the muddy slope. A short distance further, the opening came into view.

Sean steered his light into the hollow, bracing himself in case Thomas came darting out. But the passageway appeared empty, with only darkness lurking beyond the reach of his light beam.

He placed the lamp inside the opening and grasped the rope with both hands. After pulling it taut, he yanked twice. Two tugs from the other end followed, signaling Tessa's acknowledgment that he had found the tunnel.

Sean felt his pulse quicken as he willed himself into the hole. Just inside, he faltered, questioning if he was up to the mission. He *had* to be, though. The others were counting on him. If he came through for them, they'd come through for him. Unfortunately, *his* duty came first. Anyway, if he chickened out, how would he ever face them? Especially Heather. *Quit thinking about it.*

He picked up the lamp and compelled himself down the length of the passage.

Before long, the rope caught, sending him into a brief panic. *Is it too short?* Sean thought back on their preparations and assured himself, *No way.* The longest length he could find was 500 feet, and when he had analyzed the topology using a map, he concluded it would suffice. He gave it a firm jerk, freeing it from whatever it was caught on, and with a swell of relief, he continued on his way.

After spotting the shimmer of the reflection off the surface, Sean headed for it, easing up as he closed in. He broke through tentatively, pausing to scan his new surroundings while bobbing on the surface.

Although he discovered no surprises above the water, his machine gun heartbeat persisted. The last time he came here, everything had been foreign, and the fear of the unknown had filled his thoughts. This time, Sean understood where he was, and what drove his anxiety was the fear of what he *knew* lay ahead.

Fighting to ignore his rocketing pulse, he stabbed the stake into the clay and slid the carabiner over it, fixing the end of the rope just below the surface.

He squirmed up the dry section of the incline, heading toward the spot where the pitch leveled. *Keep going,* he told himself, dragging his heavy limbs up the slope.

When Sean reached the crest of the tunnel, he hesitated, then peeked over. *Nothing strange.* But then he thought about it and corrected himself: *Everything is strange.* This *whole thing* is wrong. *Shut up,* he commanded. *You're almost there. Keep going.*

He spied the stretch ahead, spotting where the walls widened into the chamber, and crawled forward.

As he drew in on the opening, Sean held up once more. *Turn back,* a voice inside his head told him. *This is crazy.* He wavered, weighing what that voice was saying against what he knew Karl would say.

When they were kids, Karl had taken to jumping off the high dive at the Clarkton swimming hole. He kept pressuring Sean to give it a try. Eventually, Sean caved in. When he got up there, it looked *so* much higher than it had from the ground. Climbing down wasn't an option, though. There was no turning back.

Here he was, standing on that high dive once again. It was ten times higher now, though.

It took everything in him, but Sean swallowed the lump lodged in his throat and pressed on.

Chapter 19

At the chamber's entrance, Sean slid his mask onto his forehead. Fighting the queasy feeling growing in his gut, he scanned the interior, taking in the sight of the bones protruding from the ceiling. Between them, vast numbers of earthworms wriggled out from the canopy before sucking back into the clay.

Pushing onto his knees and leaning forward, he shone the light into the trench at the center. Thomas lay motionless, appearing just as he had last seen him. Sean didn't know whether he should feel despair because the body was there, or relieved it hadn't gone missing.

He pushed himself forward, creeping reluctantly toward the very thing that repulsed him while being mindful to stay low, clear of the worm-infested ceiling.

The closer Sean got to Thomas, the higher his tension ratcheted. When he was within arm's reach, his body felt like it was freezing up, his tendons creaking in resistance. The tremor in his hands caused the light to quiver, jiggling the shadows and heightening his feeling of disorientation. He set the dive light on the ground.

Working from a low crouch, Sean detached the rescue harness from his belt and laid it out, arranging the straps until they were oriented the right way. *Now, for the hard part,* he thought as he turned his eyes to Thomas, averting his gaze from that wound stretching from the crown to the back of his head.

The rest of the world melted away as Sean pressed one quivering hand on the dive knife's handle, extending his other to touch Thomas's back. When he noticed a charred outline on the strange cloth, the memory of that Roman candle fireball hitting Thomas in the back flashed in his mind. He felt the rough cloth and pressed until his trembling fingertips met solid resistance.

Sean nudged Thomas as though he was attempting to rouse him, then jerked his hand back and watched as the torso shifted in the way of a lifeless object. Time froze as he waited with his hand on the dive knife, feeling his eyeballs throb in sync with his heartbeat. Thomas remained still.

A firmer shake yielded the same result.

Sean had questioned whether jostling the corpse might awaken him, but Tessa and Mildred were confident it wouldn't.

If they had been wrong, Sean was to abort. They'd regroup and figure out another plan. But they'd been correct, after all. *He's lifeless,* a little voice in Sean's mind said. *So, get on with it.*

After a long moment, Sean took a deep breath, picked up the harness, and arranged it over Thomas's back. He paused to crack his knuckles while psyching himself up for what he had to do next.

Okay, on the count of three. One. Two. Three.

With his teeth clenched on the mouthpiece, Sean slid one hand under Thomas's waist and lifted. It shocked him how light and flaccid the body felt, unlike anything alive could ever be. He shivered with the thought and used his other hand to push one end of the waist strap underneath.

Dropping the body, Sean pulled back to collect himself. Buoyed by a small feeling of having made progress, he prodded himself to continue. With a nod, he draped the opposing end over Thomas, aligned the two halves, and clicked the buckle together. *Snap.*

Next came the shoulder straps. With Thomas on his side, Sean hung one strap over the exposed shoulder and buckled it to the waist. He leaned away and stared at the smothered shoulder, still averting his eyes from the back of Thomas's head.

On three. One. Two. Three.

Sean forced himself to tilt forward. He caught a close-up look at Thomas's face, shriveled, like one of those shrunken apple-head dolls his grandmother kept in her dining room. As a child, those frightening little old ladies had provoked nightmares, and now, a life-sized one lay before him.

Sean wrinkled his nose in disgust and turned his gaze away. He slid his fingers under Thomas's head, trying not to react to the feel of it, and lifted it off his shoulder. The neck creaked, startling Sean so severely that he almost let go. But he held his position, and, using the other hand, threaded the second strap over Thomas's underneath shoulder.

When Sean lowered Thomas's head, the neck creaked once again. He took a breath and buckled the second shoulder strap, then attached the chest strap, locking the turtle shell necklace underneath the harness.

Three down, two to go. The worst two, that is.

Without allowing himself to reconsider what he was about to do, Sean lifted Thomas's leg and wrapped the strap around his thigh, cringing at the feel of the emaciated limb. He squeezed his eyes shut as he clicked the buckle together near Thomas's groin and cinched the strap tight.

Four down, one to go. Saving the worst for last. Because there's only one thing more awful than touching a mummified corpse, and that would be touching a mummified corpse between the legs.

Sean sorted out his next steps. With Thomas on his side, he would need to be raised at the hips so the second leg strap could be threaded underneath. Sean reached around and slid one hand under Thomas's hip, then lifted, grunting not because of the weight, but from the overwhelming feeling of revulsion.

After passing the strap through the gap, he lowered the body and quickly poked the other end between Thomas's legs, groaning as he did so. He mated the two ends, snapped the buckle closed, and backed away to recover.

Okay, let's jet now, Sean said to himself. *Get the hell out of here, once and for all.*

He backed up toward the tunnel, set the dive light as close to the opening as he could reach, placed his hands on Thomas above his leather foot wrappings, and took hold of the bony ankles. With a steady pull, Thomas flopped onto his back, concealing the hideous head wound, but revealing that shriveled-apple face.

Sean fought the urge to look away. He studied Thomas for the slightest movement, but there was none. He scooted back, retook hold, and tugged, dragging Thomas out from the trench.

After repositioning the lamp, Sean repeated the pattern. Crawl backward, grab, pull, and then pause for a breath (while watching for movement). Back up, grab, pull, and pause. Thomas was so light that moving him took little effort, but the trick was doing it from a crawling position, without brushing his head against the ceiling.

When he reached the smaller tunnel aperture, he waited, knowing the trick was about to become trickier.

Sean placed the dive light on top of Thomas's legs, but since he was now fully convinced Thomas wasn't moving, he oriented it toward himself so he wouldn't have to look at the gruesome figure. The spotlight on his face blinded him, but it beat the alternative.

As he inched down the tunnel, his tanks bumped into the walls, first on one side, then the other. He felt like a blind weasel trying to navigate backward through its tunnels.

When the passage began sloping downward, gravity made the undertaking slightly easier. Before long, he arrived at the waterline.

Sean replaced his mask and wiggled into the water. He dug his knees into the clay to hold himself aloft and then fumbled around underwater, searching for the stake. When his hand fell on it, he yanked it out of the clay. With the end of the rope free, he stabbed the stake into the tunnel wall above the water's surface.

Next, Sean pulled Thomas down the slope until his feet were submerged. He removed the dive lamp from where he'd perched it atop the bony legs, hung it on the stake, then steeled himself for what would follow.

After drawing a deep breath from the air tank, Sean pulled Thomas down further, steering his legs into the water and down the gap between his own lower body and the wall.

Sean then crawled up, wincing as he hovered over Thomas's scrawny midsection. He propped himself up on his elbows. With trembling hands, he attached the carabiner to the hook in the center of the safety harness. Holding himself away from the body in a modified one-arm push-up, he reached down, pulled the rope taut, and gave it three sharp tugs.

A moment later, the rope jerked back three times, drew taut, and began dragging Thomas downward. Sean held himself clear as

Thomas slid into the water and sank, bubbles rising on the surface where he disappeared.

Tension drained out of Sean's body. Although the task wasn't over, he had cleared the worst part.

Sean twisted around until he was facing head down, pulled the dive light from the stake, and shimmied into the water.

Once submerged, he struggled to get his bearings in the nearly opaque water. When he eventually caught a glimpse of how Thomas was moving through the passage, he understood why the water was so turbid. Being towed feet-first, Thomas's limbs were scissoring out from the center of his torso, scraping against the walls, stirring up silt clouds.

Sean regretted not having oriented Thomas in a head-first direction, and as he kicked to catch up to Thomas, he considered whether it was too late to turn him around. Before he could decide, Thomas's foot caught on the passageway's wall, pretzeling his leg up and in, folding it against his body. Thomas's torso tucked and pivoted, and his upper back bumped into the opposite wall, thickening the murk with a new bloom of silt.

Sean closed in. He used his light to probe the mushrooming cloud, searching for anything visible, but finding nothing. Without stopping to think about it, he extended his free hand into the haze and groped around. His fingers caught on something stringy, and the instant he realized it was hair, his fingertips embedded into a spongy surface. He jerked his hand away, realizing he'd planted it on that gruesome wound. Strands of hair tore off Thomas's head, tangling between Sean's fingers.

Sean shivered as he shook his fingers free, but he told himself to stay calm, knowing he couldn't afford to freak out. He adjusted his bearings and aimed his hand where he imagined Thomas's chest would be. Sure enough, his fingers landed on the metal loop where the rope was attached to the safety harness. The line was taut, straining without effect.

The murkiness gradually thinned. As Heather and Tessa continued tugging on the rope, Thomas's leg bent further up while his torso scrunched into an angular contortion, taking on a crooked C shape, lodged across the width of the passageway. Sean groaned at the sight and wondered if the women pulled hard enough, could they tear Thomas's fragile, withered body apart? *God, this is* so *warped.*

The line yanked forcefully on the harness, but the wedged body didn't budge.

Out of nowhere, an even more panic-inducing question popped into Sean's head. Was Thomas's body blocking Sean's escape? Through the haze, he examined the narrow space between Thomas and the top of the tunnel, straining to judge whether the gap was wide enough for him to worm through. Definitely not with the tanks attached to his back—and removing them would be perilous.

Get him turned around!

He kicked forward, stopping his momentum with an open palm against Thomas's sternum. He dropped the dive light and grabbed the bent leg with one arm while pushing on Thomas's shoulder with the other, bracing his own knees against the tunnel's wall for leverage.

With all his might, Sean wrenched on Thomas's body. Even underwater, he heard Thomas's hip shatter.

Thomas crumpled into a tighter tuck, turned, and began pulling away, moving head-first down the passage. A wave of relief washed over Sean. He retrieved the dive light and propelled himself forward, following closely behind, the water's inkiness clearing as they proceeded into undisturbed water.

What Sean saw next made his heart leap.

Thomas had opened his eyes.

It was just a brief glimpse, cut short by their shifting positions, but Sean would have sworn that's what he'd seen. He aimed the light at Thomas's head and watched, waiting for Thomas's face to tilt back his way. When it did, Sean reeled back. What he saw was unmistakable and shocking: Thomas glowered at him with those horrible, reddish eyes.

Sean caught hold of the tunnel wall to slow his momentum, allowing Thomas to be towed away. As he drifted out toward the beacon of daylight where the tunnel opened into the river, Thomas's head swayed limply with the current, giving brief flashes of eye contact. Sean's scalp prickled each time, with only the growing distance between them lessening his anguish.

Had Thomas...woken up? Like...risen from the dead? What was next? Would he start *moving?*

Sean's stomach curdled as the questions flitted through his brain.

While he watched Thomas recede in the distance, his distress lessened, until a new, even more disturbing, thought sparked inside his mind.

I've got to warn them!

Chapter 20

SEAN KICKED FRANTICALLY, AIMING for the opening Thomas had just passed through. As he proceeded down the tunnel, he imagined Heather and Tessa on the riverbank, reeling in the rope, and, just as Thomas surfaced, he'd surge out of the water, pouncing on one of them.

Sean shot out of the tunnel and into the river. He swept over his surroundings with the light beam, spotting Thomas, whose dead weight had carried him downstream with the current. Sean immediately saw how this would give him an advantage. He'd get there first if he kept his pace and followed a straight line across the river. As he labored, Sean stole glimpses of Thomas, flopping on the rope's end as the women hauled him through the water.

But the way Thomas was whipping around like a lure on the end of the fishing line...was his limp body merely undulating with the flow? Or was he moving—*writhing*—on his own power? It was hard to say.

Sean tightened his form to streamline his movement and kicked furiously. *Go! Go! Go!* Soon, his dive light fell on the opposite bank, revealing the finish line he'd been looking for. He focused on it and watched it grow closer, aiming underneath the taut rope angling into the water.

Thomas's squirming form appeared in Sean's peripheral vision. Although he drew nearer with every second, he lagged far enough behind to convince Sean they weren't on a collision path.

Sean aimed for the surface and blasted through, hurling himself onto the shore. He scooted into a seated position on the bank, ripped off his mask, and spat out the mouthpiece. "He's alive!" As the words came out, he realized they weren't quite right, but it was the best he could do in the panicked moment.

Stationed beside one another, holding the rope, Heather and Tessa wore identical expressions, their heads cocked and their mouths hanging open.

The sound of a splash tore their attention away. In unison, all three heads wheeled to face it. Downriver, two scraggy arms had broken through the surface, fifteen feet from Sean. Thomas's gaunt face rose from the water, and his dreadful, glowing eyes immediately homed in on Sean.

Sean kicked off his fins, wiggled the tanks off his shoulders, and unbuckled the weight belt. He detached the dive knife, palmed it, and then rolled onto his feet, struggling to steady himself on legs made of Silly Putty.

Although Thomas was within an arm's length of the water's edge, he mostly remained submerged. Sean stared at him, questioning why he wasn't standing. The water would be only waist-deep at that spot. All of a sudden, the explanation came to him. "His hip's broken!"

Heather and Tessa kept their gapes fixed on Thomas, but Heather managed to say, "Huh?"

"I'll explain later." Sean turned back to Thomas.

With the grace of a hobbled dog trying to work its way out of the river, Thomas was nearing the water's edge.

Sean scanned the stone wall atop the opposite bank and was relieved to see nobody there. If anyone witnessed this ghastly sight, their plan would be jeopardized. The risk of that would soon drop, though. As Thomas proceeded toward them, leaf cover would obscure him to any passersby.

Thomas reached for dry ground with one hand, then the other. He pulled, drawing himself to the bank. His torso rose from the river, water pouring off the safety harness and his primitive shirt. One leg thrust him forward, while the other dangled uselessly. He collapsed on the ground, with his lower legs still in the water, then shoved his upper body up from the surface, as if doing a pushup.

The sight of the rope hanging slack from Thomas's chest broke Sean's trance, prompting him to turn back to the women. They stood frozen, their eyes as wide as doughnuts, the line sagging in their hands.

Sean lunged for the rope near their feet, snatched a furl, and unspooled it from the coil. He formed a loop and tried to slice through it with the knife. "Damn!" he yelled, realizing it wasn't going to be so easy to cut through.

"I'll hold it!" Heather grabbed the rope and clutched it firmly. "You cut with two hands."

Seizing the knife in both hands, Sean sawed feverishly on the loop. He broke his concentration when the fibers finally began fraying. Over Heather's shoulder, Sean watched Thomas squirm-crawling up the embankment, plodding forward with each shove of his functional leg. He was not moving quickly. That shattered hip gave them a chance.

The cutting action seemed to increase during the last few strokes, and the knife broke through with a gratifying release. Sean grabbed the segment attached to Thomas and raced partway up the slope, wrapping it behind a solid tree trunk before pulling it taut. Heather and Tessa, seemingly reading his mind, scurried to assist, taking a position on the section of rope between Thomas and the tree.

"On three!" Sean yelled. "One, two, three!" They dragged Thomas up the slope a body length using a strong, unified heave.

As if Thomas realized what was happening, he dug his hands and knee into the soil and leaned against the force to fight against being towed further.

In turn, Sean coiled the rope around his arm for a better grip. "One, two, three!"

They hoisted Thomas further up the embankment, leaving furrows in the ground where he had fastened himself.

"One, two, three!"

As their tug tapered off this time, Thomas lunged toward Heather's legs. She sprang out of his reach, and he fell harmlessly on the ground.

"Move over here!" Sean hollered as he choked up on the segment of rope that had lengthened considerably beyond the trunk, pulling it tight once again.

The women hurried around the tree, took their new positions in front of Sean, and grabbed hold.

"One, two, three!"

That drag cut the remaining distance between Thomas and the tree in half.

"One more pull and he'll be pinned to the tree!" Heather said.

Sean nodded. It was exactly what he had been figuring. Without giving Thomas time to maneuver, Sean repeated his chant. "One, two, three!"

Their final yank lugged Thomas against the tree trunk, chest-first. His head writhed as he struggled to pull free, but Sean acted quickly.

He took the rope from the women, and, holding it taut, circled behind his captive, wrapping it over Thomas's torso and cinching it. He dashed around the tree three more times, binding Thomas against it. Although Thomas's arms were free, his torso was moored tightly to the trunk.

Heather gave Sean a Rocky Balboa pose. "Clutch move, homeboy."

Sean smiled awkwardly but felt his cheeks growing warm, so he went to work tethering the rope's end to the closest tree, giving him a good reason to face away.

"You said he was dormant," Tessa said, slowly wiping one palm across her forehead.

Sean got momentarily hung up on that word. *Dormant.* That wasn't the word he'd used. He'd said "inert," a word they used in biology. And chemistry. However, he had to admit that "dormant" was probably a better fit with the context. "I said *inert.*"

Tessa held her hands out, palms up. "Okay. But I wouldn't call *that...*" She tossed her head at Thomas. "...dormant *or* inert."

"Fair enough." Sean motioned for them to follow, leading them away until he was sure they were out of Thomas's earshot. *Just in case it matters.* He leaned in and spoke in a hushed tone. "He *was* dormant—*inert*—whatever, inside the chamber. But he opened his eyes after I put him in the water."

Tessa screwed up her face and turned away to face the river.

Heather covered her mouth with her palm and knitted her brow. "Like the water...*resurrected* him?"

Tessa bowed her head and bit her lower lip as she processed this. Then she inhaled audibly as she lifted her chin. "Water is life."

Sean flicked his eyes at Heather, giving her an almost imperceptible facial-movement shrug. When Heather responded with nothing but a blank stare, Sean continued. "Anyway, he got all jammed up in the tunnel, and I broke his hip trying to get him unstuck. By the time he reached this side of the river, he was moving."

Tessa remained facing the river. Sean studied the bear's claw tattoo beside her eye and cracked his knuckles while waiting for her to say something. When he finished, but she still hadn't spoken, he stepped squarely into her field of view. "So, what do we do now?"

Tessa puckered her lips in a frown.

Sean peered over his shoulder. Thomas was chafing against the tree with his untethered arms, causing a faint scratching sound, but he remained thoroughly shackled.

"We need to stick with the plan," Tessa eventually said. "Take him to the deadhouse."

"Like this?" Heather asked, turning her eyes to Thomas.

"We'll tie him up before we hide him in the kayak." Tessa pointed her thumb over her shoulder at the fiberglass kayak they'd carried to this spot. "I hate to do that, but we have no choice."

Sean tried to picture Thomas, all bound up and tucked in the bottom of the vessel—*like a coffin disguised as a kayak.* Sean shook his head, clearing the ghastly image.

Heather sighed, breaking the silence. "Ready?"

Tessa nodded, then Sean.

The rustling sound grew louder as Thomas wriggled in vain against the tree trunk.

Sean took a deep breath, turned, and headed his way.

After cutting off three more rope segments, one longer length plus two shorter ones, Sean kneeled behind Thomas's feet. While

Thomas's unbroken leg kicked at him, the crippled limb, twisted out of alignment, merely twitched.

Sean grimaced and averted his gaze. He held up one short length of cord. "I'll lash his ankles together first."

Heather and Tessa dropped to either side and took hold of Thomas's good leg. He kicked defiantly, but when they leaned into him, they were able to anchor the leg to the ground.

Sean tethered the rope around the leathery ankle, leaving a free stretch to tie off the other end. He then wrapped the cording around both ankles, cinching each loop tight before securing it with a square knot.

"Wrists next?" Heather asked.

"For sure," Sean said, and they all moved to the other side of the tree.

Sean scratched his head as he studied how Thomas's arms were fixed on opposite sides of the trunk.

Before he could say anything, Heather beat him to it. "We've got to release him to free his arms."

Sean gave the okay sign, and while she moved over to where he had secured the rope's end, he picked up the second shorter segment. "Before you undo that knot, let me tie this to one wrist first." Thomas struggled against him, but since he was so well restrained, he could do little to prevent Sean from binding the cording to his wrist.

"All set," Sean said, giving Heather a head nod.

She unwound the rope, and Thomas collapsed onto his side. Heather scrambled to join Tessa in clamping Thomas's other forearm while Sean lashed the rope around both wrists.

Once the wrists were bound, all three rose to their feet and paused to catch their breath. Thomas wriggled futilely, face up. He glared at each of them in turns, his mouth snapping open and closed, looking like a fish out of water.

"Now we'll bind his arms to his body." Sean picked up the longer length of rope, crouched over Thomas, grabbed him behind his shoulder, and pulled him up into a seated position.

Without warning, Thomas's head twisted, and before Sean could react, a flare of pain soon shot through his forearm. Sean yanked his arm away but felt a tearing sensation as he ripped free from Thomas's bite.

He grabbed his wounded arm and watched in shock as blood bloomed from one of the tooth marks. Rage overcame him. He kicked Thomas, knocking him back to the ground. "You sonofabitch!"

Tessa grabbed Sean and held him back, boring into him with a frosty glare. "Stop it!"

Sean pulled away and pointed to his arm. "He bit me."

"I know. I saw it. You know he's not a zombie, right?"

"Yeah, I know that." In truth, it helped to be reminded because *Night of the Living Dead* was the first thing that had flashed through Sean's mind. But still, he didn't need to be embarrassed in front of Heather.

"Don't be a stupid settler," Tessa said.

Sean scrunched up his face. *Settler?* He had to think about what that meant, but then it came to him. He looked at Heather, who responded with a subtle facial shrug.

"Sorry, I shouldn't have called you that."

He gave a weak "no big deal" headshake, deciding she was acting protective of Thomas, that's all.

When Sean prodded the wound with his index finger, he realized it wasn't the most vicious bite imaginable. It was more the injustice of it all that had him torqued.

Heather stepped forward and inspected Sean's arm. She gave no reaction, which he took to mean she thought he had nothing to worry about.

"Do either of you have a dog?"

Sean did a double-take, raising an eyebrow at Tessa.

"*I* do," Heather said. "Ralphie. He's a miniature dachshund."

Tessa's face softened. The corner of her lips turned upward slightly until she seemed to catch herself, clearing her expression. Maybe she thought a wiener dog didn't qualify, never mind the miniature part. She turned her eyes to Sean.

He shook his head, not bothering to mention his mom's allergies.

"Do you know why dogs bite?"

Sean froze, thinking, *Because they're mean?*

But Heather answered without hesitation. "Because they're scared."

"That's right," Tessa said. "I know it's difficult, but try to think about what Thomas is going through. Let's control our emotions. Stay focused on our objective."

Sean turned back to Thomas and watched him straining against the lashings.

"I have an idea," Heather said.

Sean and Tessa turned to her.

"Let's cover his head with your wetsuit."

Sean squinted at her, then looked down at the neoprene material. He pinched the thick foam rubber while chewing the inside of his cheek. "Actually, that's an awesome idea. It's about time for me to put on dry clothes, anyway." He turned to Tessa for approval.

Tessa sighed. "Okay."

Sean wandered over to his bag and fished out his clothes and a hand towel. He squirmed out of the wetsuit, dried himself off, and dressed, pulling his jeans over his still-wet swimsuit.

As he headed back to the others, he turned the wetsuit over, trying to determine the best way to orient it. He zipped it up halfway, kneeled beside Thomas, and then pulled the suit over Thomas's head, facing backward and upside-down. Thomas snarled.

"You asked for it," Sean told him. Then he turned to Heather. "It's a good look on him, don't you think?"

Heather didn't take the bait, though.

Tessa shot Sean a dirty look. She stooped down, placed her hands on Thomas's head, and spoke a few words Sean didn't recognize. Before long, Thomas relaxed, just slightly.

"Let's try this again." Sean leaned over Thomas and cautiously pulled him upright.

When Thomas lifted his arms as if preparing to swing them, Heather and Tessa crouched to restrain them, pinning them firmly to his lap.

Sean released the carabiner from the safety harness and replaced it with the new rope segment, securing it with a double half-hitch knot. He left some extra length to tie off to, then wrapped Thomas's torso repeatedly, binding his arms. He encircled the wetsuit around Thomas's neck, cinched the rope, and tied it off at the chest.

All three of them stood and looked over their captive, all bound up like an Egyptian mummy, ready to be inserted into its sarcophagus.

Sean was the first to break the huddle. He walked over to the kayak, yanked the seat out of the opening, and placed it on the ground. "Should we put him in head first, or feet first?"

Chapter 21

HALFWAY ACROSS THE FIELD, Sean's shoulder muscles were burning. Since he did not want to be the one to request a break, he was grateful when Tessa asked for one.

"I should have brought my grandparents to help lug this stuff," Tessa said as they placed the kayak between the crop rows.

While Heather hurried to catch up, Sean wiped the sweat from his forehead. "We might have ended up carrying them, too."

"Hmmm. Good point." Tessa cleared the loose strands of hair from her face.

Sean examined the bite on his forearm, prodding the area with his thumb to gauge the pain. It was now little more than a dull ache, and the blood had clotted.

"It's nothing to worry about," Tessa told him.

Sean nodded promptly, like she'd said something he already knew.

Heather arrived, dropping the scuba gear and the coil of rope. She and Tessa had taken turns carrying the boat's bow end for each quarter of the jaunt. "I'm so worried Grand-Bob will get suspicious."

Sean glanced at the mobile home. "No way. I'm telling you: he was totally pumped when I told him we'd be using Karl's kayak. It hasn't been touched in that storage shed since Karl died." He turned to face Tessa. "Sorry, I meant the deadhouse."

Tessa bobbed her head from side to side. "It's a shed, for sure. But until tonight, it's our makeshift deadhouse, too."

Heather asked, "And you're sure Grand-Bob can't get in there?"

"Most definitely. He hasn't used that shed in years. It was empty when Karl and I put the kayak in there, and we used my padlock. I know Grand-Bob never had the combination, because Karl stashed his pot in there."

"Hope you're right," Tessa said. "At least until after dark, when we remove him."

The vessel rocked gently as Thomas, hidden in the bottom underneath the seat, struggled against his restraints. All three of them stared at the swaying boat until Heather interrupted the macabre sight. "So, what is this stuff?" She pointed at the crop.

"Soybeans," Sean said.

"I thought they grew corn here."

"They do. Farmers rotate to improve the soil and fight pests."

"Hmmm." With her distraction tactic successfully executed, Heather seemed to lose whatever interest she might've had in the subject. She positioned herself at the bow. "It's my turn to portage, Tessa."

Sean smiled at how she pronounced it: por-*tazh,* with an emphasis on the second syllable. "I think you've taken too many of those French classes."

Heather air-chuckled, as if reluctant to express too much humor amid the grim situation. She grabbed the handle on her end. "My turn to portage." This time, she said it like por-tij, without the emphasis. She gave Sean a slightly playful look.

He grinned, turned, and lifted the stern.

Thomas was inhumanly light, so the total weight was easily manageable initially. But it sure seemed to grow heavier as they proceeded across the field.

They stopped for one more break, and afterward, Tessa carried the bow end while Heather took over lugging the other gear.

The rear door swung open when the trio crossed from the field's end row into Grand-Bob's backyard.

"Howdy, Buttercup." Grand-Bob stepped out in his bathrobe, despite it being afternoon. "You've got *two* girlfriends now?"

They put the kayak down in the grass. "Two *friends.* You remember Heather?"

Heather waved, and Grand-Bob nodded.

"And that's Tessa," Heather added, pointing with her thumb.

Tessa lifted her chin.

Pleased to meet you," Grand-Bob said. "How was the boating?"

"Great," Sean said, a bit too quickly. The kayak rocked, so he leaned against it with his lower leg to hold it steady.

Tessa clamped the point of the bow between her calves.

"Yeah, awesome," Heather said.

"Well, you kids are welcome to use it anytime."

"Thanks, Grand-Bob," Sean said. "We'll put it away and lock up now."

Grand-Bob gave a thumbs-up, pulled open the door, and disappeared into the house.

They hauled the kayak beyond the detached garage, stopping at the storage shed built against the side facing away from the house.

After he and Tessa put the boat on the grass, Sean started turning the combination lock dial. He spoke the numbers out loud as he dialed them in. "Twelve, twenty-four, thirty-six." Thank God the numbers were so easy to remember, all multiples of twelve. Even recalling their sequence was nothing, since they went in ascending order. The lock released with a tug.

Tessa placed the gear in the corner, switched on the battery-powered lantern, and waved Sean and Heather into the dimly lit interior. She stepped aside as Sean steered the boat through the doorway. "Put it against the wall."

While they situated the kayak along the side of the storage shed, Tessa unzipped the duffel bag she'd brought. Then she stopped and looked at Heather. "You brought the holy water, right?"

Heather reached into her jeans pocket and pulled out a small bottle. She held it out for Tessa.

Tessa leaned away. "The Christian religion is no longer practiced much in our community. You should be the one who sprinkles it on the ground."

Heather removed the cap and began drizzling the water over the gravel floor, jerking her hand to spread it around.

The kayak pitched listlessly. Sean licked his dry lips and pressed his leg against the fiberglass stern, restraining the vessel's movement.

When the bottle was empty, Heather shook out the last remaining drops, replaced the cap, and pocketed it.

Tessa stretched open the duffel bag and began removing evergreen tree boughs from it, arranging them on the floor in the middle of the shed.

"What's that for?" Heather asked.

"I'm preparing a bed for Thomas. To help him find rest." Tessa placed the last two boughs. "This is red cedar. It has medicinal properties."

Tessa stood and looked over the arrangement before turning away. She picked up the lantern and leaned over the kayak's opening, attempting to peer inside. Sean straddled the kayak and detached the seat blocking their view. Only Thomas's rope-bound midsection was visible. The vessel shook as he squirmed.

"Please remove him and place him on the cedar limbs."

Sean gritted his teeth and crouched over the opening. He grasped Thomas at the waist and slid him down until his head, shrouded by the wetsuit, was centered in the aperture. Heather sidled up beside him to assist.

Sean sucked in a deep inhale and lifted Thomas at the shoulders. Together, he and Heather snaked Thomas out of the kayak as he wiggled fruitlessly. They laid him on the red cedar boughs.

Tessa removed a small bundle from the bag and carried it to where Thomas lay. She withdrew a lighter from her pocket and lit the end of the bundle.

"What's that?" Heather asked.

"Sweetgrass," Tessa said as the dried leaves caught fire. "It's a medicinal herb we use in traditional ceremonies." She leaned over and blew out the flame, sending a swirl of smoke into the air.

Sean caught a whiff of the burning foliage, which had a vanilla scent.

Tessa slowly waved the smoking bundle over Thomas's body, then announced, "You must wait outside."

Sean and Heather traded glances. She motioned for him to follow her to the doorway.

The last thing Sean saw as he headed outside was Tessa kneeling beside Thomas, placing her free hand on his hooded head.

Heather blew out a long breath as the two of them stepped out onto the grass. "Close the shed."

As Sean closed the door behind him, he lowered his voice a notch and corrected her. "It's a deadhouse. Whatever that means."

"Yeah. A deadhouse. Tessa explained that to me on the way down."

"Fill me in."

"In the old days, Moravian Christians stored their dead in small buildings they called deadhouses, before burying them. Tessa's community has mostly abandoned the Moravian religion and returned to traditional native spiritual practices. But since this would have been the practice when Thomas lived, she thought it would help prepare him for the burial."

"Got it," Sean whispered before breaking into a grin. "Plus..." He pointed with his thumb at the Granada, parked at the dead end. "...It's better than locking him in my trunk until nighttime."

Heather raised her eyebrows hesitantly, like trying to decide whether to share in Sean's amusement. She resisted.

When Sean picked up the sound of Tessa's muffled voice, he leaned into the door and cocked his head.

"Good luck with that," Heather said in a hushed tone. "She's speaking Lunaapeew, her native language."

Sean listened as he cracked his knuckles, one finger at a time. "What do you think she's saying?"

Heather shrugged. "Maybe she's telling him he needs to move on."

After listening for a while, he asked, "So, where did you get the holy water?"

Heather gave a humorless chuckle. "St. Mary's church, off the Kent State campus. I pilfered it from one of the entrance fonts."

"Let's pray you won't burn in hell for that." Sean gave her a playful smile.

She puckered her lips. "I just hope it works. It wasn't blessed by a Moravian pastor."

"So, is this going to be a Moravian Christian burial?"

Heather shook her head. "The deadhouse is the only Moravian thing. Otherwise, this will be a traditional native burial."

They fell into an extended silence. Sean examined the bite on his forearm. Although a bruise had started to form, it really didn't look bad. *Forget about it,* he told himself.

Looking up at the mid-afternoon sky, he noticed thin, high clouds spreading overhead. *Hope it doesn't rain.* He did not say it out loud, afraid it might jinx them.

Eventually, Tessa's voice diminished, and after a spell, the shed went quiet.

Just when Sean started worrying that Grand-Bob might wonder why they hadn't left yet, the door clicked open. Tessa motioned them in.

The shed—*might as well call it the deadhouse*—was crowded with shadows. Tessa had turned off the lantern, leaving the open doorway as the only light source. While Sean waited for his eyes to adjust to the gloom, Heather gasped, then slapped her hand over her mouth as she stared wide-eyed at Thomas. Sean switched his gaze back in that direction, and when the darkened image came into view, panic shot through him.

Thomas had been untied.

The ropes and rescue harness had been removed and piled to the side. The wetsuit had been taken off his head, revealing that gaunt, leathery-skinned face in a frozen expression, mouth cocked ajar.

"You let him go?" Heather asked, her voice filled with anxiety.

Tessa nodded. "He asked me to."

Sean frowned but resisted the urge to react. "That seems like a bad idea."

Tessa held out her open hand at Thomas, showing how he lay perfectly still on the bed of cedar boughs. "His spirit is tranquil."

"Yeah," Sean said. "Maybe for now."

Tessa's eyes skirted over to Thomas. She studied him for a while before speaking. "To build trust with him, I need to consider how he feels."

She paused and turned back to face Sean and Heather. "A remnant of Thomas's spirit is stuck in our world. It doesn't belong here, but it's hanging on, caught in a cycle of vengeance. How do we break this cycle?"

Sean tried to read Tessa's expression. Was she expecting a response, or simply asking a rhetorical question?

"Through forgiveness?" Heather said it like a question, as though the teacher had put her on the spot, and she was unsure of her answer.

Tessa nodded. "Forgiveness. Trust. Empathy. The words are easy to say, but these things are hard to practice."

She turned back to Thomas. "We must reunify his spirit and get him to move on. We can only do this through forgiveness, trust, and empathy. These things start with us."

Tessa stood there silently for a spell, then moved toward the door and gestured for them to follow. Heather went first, then Sean. He glanced at Thomas one last time as he stepped through the door frame. Thomas hadn't moved.

When all three were standing on the grass, Tessa swung the door closed. "Our job here is done, for now." She placed the padlock on the door and clicked it shut. "We'll return to my grandparents while Thomas rests in the deadhouse. The medicinal herbs will help keep him tranquil."

As Tessa headed for the car with Heather following closely behind, Sean held back momentarily. He tugged the lock to confirm it was latched, then hurried to catch up.

Chapter 22

When Sean turned onto the Moravian Village Library's block, he spotted Norman and Mildred sitting on the bench near the library's entrance. Pumpkins flanked them at their feet, and the window behind them had been adorned for Halloween with cobwebs.

Tessa was the first to climb out, opening her door before Sean could put the Granada in park. "Why are you out here?" she asked from the curb.

The elders grinned. "We got tired of sitting inside," Norman said.

"It's a nice day," Mildred added.

Norman looked at the sky. "At least for now. Rain is on the way."

As they gathered on the sidewalk in front of the library, Mildred asked Tessa, "How did it go?"

Tessa took a deep breath. "He's in the deadhouse, but things didn't go as planned."

Mildred arched an eyebrow.

"Water brought him life," Tessa said.

The elderly couple turned to each other. A look passed between them. Mildred sighed, turning back to Tessa. "Yes, of course."

"Water is life," Norman said, echoing the words Tessa had spoken down by the river.

"Things got...complicated." Tessa's face went grim. "But it's okay now. Thomas is tranquil."

"Nicely done, granddaughter." Mildred placed a hand on Tessa's shoulder.

"You taught her well," Norman said to Mildred.

"She was awesome," Heather piled on.

Sean nodded.

Tessa turned to face Sean and Heather. "These kids did well. We made a good team." She looked Sean in the eyes. "Again, I'm sorry I got riled up at you."

He shrugged and grinned self-consciously. "I deserved it." In truth, that wasn't quite how Sean felt, but it seemed like the polite thing to say.

"Maybe. Maybe not." Tessa patted him on the shoulder. "But our entire plan started with you, and you came through."

Sean felt himself blushing, but fortunately, a man walking his German shepherd came strolling through. The gathering shifted off the sidewalk to make room, but the dog beelined toward Norman, pulling the leash taut and greeting him with a rapid-fire tail wag.

"Well, hello there, boy." Norman crouched down and, with a steady movement, began petting the shepherd on his side.

Tessa grinned at Heather and Sean. "All dogs love my grandfather."

The shepherd dropped to the sidewalk and rolled onto his back.

"Oh, come on, Felix," the man said, shaking his head. Then, to Norman, he said, "Sorry."

Norman chuckled, gave Felix's belly a few rubs, then pushed himself back up with a groan. Felix rolled back over, righted himself, and hurried after his owner as he led him away.

When the man was out of earshot, Tessa turned to her grandparents. "We have four hours before it gets dark. It's almost a half-hour drive to the motel each way, but that still leaves us three hours. Should we go check in?"

Only four hours, Sean thought, feeling like he needed a longer break than that to recover from the gut-wrenching events of the afternoon. *Like a week. Better yet, a month.* But the plan was underway, and there was no going back now, so tonight was the night.

"I wouldn't mind a nap," Norman said with a smiling wink, but looking like he really meant it.

"Me too," Mildred added.

"Okay, then," Tessa said. "It's nap time." She shrugged at Sean. "We hit the road early this morning."

Sean felt comforted by their lighthearted demeanors. It made him feel he shouldn't dread what lay ahead so much.

Tessa turned to Heather. "Hey, roommate, I could check into our room and take your overnight bag, if you prefer hanging around here."

When Heather's eyes ticked toward Sean, he responded quickly. "The doughnut shop is open until six. I have the munchies anyway. Afterward, I could show you some cool things in the area."

Heather flashed a thumbs-up.

"Don't eat too much," Mildred said. "Save room for the feast."

"I'll keep him on a restricted diet," Heather said.

"It will be dark by eight o'clock," Tessa said over her shoulder as she stepped over to the Volkswagen Bus and opened its rear door for her grandparents. "Let's meet then, back here."

Sean gave her the "okay" hand gesture before turning and following Heather down the sidewalk toward the town square.

When Sean caught up to Heather, she wagged a finger. "I have an idea. How about we split a sandwich?"

"Is this part of that restricted diet thing?"

She nodded. "Ham and Swiss, or roast beast and cheddar?"

"How about ham and cheddar?" he offered. "Or roast beast and Swiss?"

"Hmmm...a compromise." Heather bobbed her head. "You pick."

Sean scooted ahead to hold open the door.

"Always the gentleman," Heather said with a smile.

Summoned by the jingle of the door's bell, Big Boy emerged from the back. He grinned enthusiastically, as if he remembered them. Although they *had* become regulars, this would be their last visit if everything went as planned.

Sean ordered a ham and Swiss cheese sandwich, offering Heather a coy look in response to the surprised expression painted on her face.

"And we'd like six apple fritters in a to-go box," Heather told the man. "For the feast," she said to Sean in a whisper.

As the Big Boy doughnut man went to work on their order, Sean and Heather headed for the tables. Heather pointed with her open hand. "The usual?"

"Of course," Sean said. "Best seat in the house."

When they settled at the table, Sean popped open his can of root beer. He wanted to ask Heather about the no-more-boyfriend bombshell, but couldn't devise a smooth way to bring it up.

Instead, he decided to stick with the day's events. "Would anyone believe what we just went through?"

Heather shook her head. "No effin' way."

"It's a total trip if you stop and think about it."

"I'm trying not to," Heather said.

"Good idea." Sean examined the bite on his arm. The bruise had darkened and spread, but the skin tear didn't look like much to worry about. "I'm nervous about tonight."

"Most definitely." Heather opened her can of 7 Up. "If it's anything like this afternoon, it's going to be a wild ride."

"I hope these people know what they're doing."

"I'm sure they do." She took a swig. "Anyway, they'd better. They're our only chance."

Sean sipped his root beer and considered this. "I know. I keep thinking: What would we do if we didn't have them?"

Big Boy arrived with their tray. Heather put the Moravi-Yum Donuts box on the window ledge, placed half the sandwich on her napkin, and slid the plate with the other half over to Sean.

Although Sean attempted to pace himself, he had little success. Soon, he'd scarfed down the last of his share, but he felt hungrier than ever, as though the tiny morsel had merely stimulated his appetite. Determined not to complain, he sat back and cracked his knuckles. "So, what's this feast all about?"

Heather finished chewing and wiped her mouth before answering. "This is an important part of the ceremony. The burial is concluded with a feast. They brought traditionally prepared food. Corn soup. Wild meat. Cornbread."

Sean pointed at the doughnut box with his chin. "Don't forget the apple fritters."

"Good point. That's *our* contribution." Heather took a sip of her pop. "A plate with a little of everything will be set aside for Thomas. This will be his last meal, to prepare his spirit for the journey."

As Sean thought about the feast, Heather's lower leg brushed against his. He almost moved away, but stopped himself. Expecting her to pull back, he froze when she didn't, and his full attention focused on the pleasing sensation.

Heather nibbled on her sandwich, then examined it, licking her lips. Did she realize her leg was leaning against his? Maybe she thought it was the leg of the table. But he could feel the warmth of her touch, so wouldn't his leg feel warm to her?

He shifted slightly, not enough to jostle her, but enough to signal she wasn't touching the table. She didn't withdraw. If anything, she leaned in closer.

"We'll be eating cold food," she said, jarring Sean away from the questions whipping him into a frenzy.

What were we talking about? Oh, yeah. The feast. Cold food. "Hey, I'm a college student. I'm used to eating cold food."

Heather's leg pressed in. Her eyes met his. "Even soup?"

Sean made a show of contemplating this while applying gentle pressure in return. "As hungry as I am, it doesn't sound bad."

Heather adjusted in her seat, and her other leg brushed against the opposite side of his calf, sandwiching him, doubling the electric feeling.

The amber color of her eyes drew him in. "Normally, the feast is cooked over a nearby fire."

Sean strained to redirect his thoughts to the conversation. What did she say? He played back her words. *Normally, the feast is cooked over a nearby fire.* He forced himself to formulate a response. "We can't exactly have a fire in the graveyard."

A smile played on Heather's lips, which made Sean feel like he was melting. What was *she* feeling?

In the past, there had been moments when Sean suspected she might have been flirting, but he was terrible at reading these types of things. Plus, she was out of his league, so chances were, it had been wishful thinking.

She was probably smiling now because he had stated the obvious. *We can't exactly have a fire in the graveyard.* He *had* stated the obvious.

She squeezed, clamping his leg. "Tessa thinks it would be okay to alter that part of the ceremony."

What part? Sean's heart was pumping hard. *Oh yeah, forgoing the fire.* He knew he should say something, but with the incredible sensation of Heather's touch, he was lost for words. He gazed into her eyes.

The bell on the door rang, and a child blurted out, "I want a pink one!"

An even younger voice said, "I wanna jelly-filled!"

Heather's eyes turned away. She sat up straight, pulled her legs back, and turned to face the interlopers.

Sean craned his neck. A woman with two young children traipsed over to the counter. He turned to face Heather and watched as she pushed the last piece of her sandwich into her mouth. She chewed it slowly while she stared out the window, seemingly focused on nothing.

"The time of day is another modification," she eventually said. "Burial ceremonies are supposed to be done in daylight."

"I wish."

Heather turned and faced him with a questioning look. "You wish?"

“I wish the burial could be done in daylight.”

Heather nodded, then turned back to face the window. “Don’t we all.”

Chapter 23

By the time Sean drove back into Moravian Village, the last of dusk was fading into complete darkness. With almost two hours to kill between the doughnut shop closing and the reunion with Tessa and her grandparents, Sean had taken Heather on a cruise across Homer County.

He'd shown her both haunted houses her mother had written about: The Harmon Manor, commonly known as "Misery Mansion," and The Gould Homestead, nicknamed "Ghoul House." In between, they'd passed through Clarkton and caught views of the tallest point in the County, Kassel's Hill, which Sean and Karl had once climbed.

Heather had gotten a kick out of seeing the Amish when they passed through the parts of the county where they had settled. People outside Homer County seemed to find the Amish so fascinating, but they had always been just another part of the local scene to Sean, so he never understood the fuss.

Although Heather seemed interested in the tour, Sean did not feel any of the energy they had shared in the doughnut shop. Either the moment had passed, or he'd misinterpreted incidental contact as something more. Probably the latter.

With the distraction over, the memory of what they faced after sunset rushed back into Sean's consciousness. A feeling of dread steadily mushroomed within his chest as the anticipation weighed on him. But neither of them spoke about it.

"Hey, what did you think of Tessa calling you a 'settler?'" Heather asked.

Sean made a cringy face. "I guess it's better than 'paleface.' Right?"

"I'm not sure about that," Heather said with a smirk.

"It's kind of weird, to be honest. I mean, I understand her beef, but all four of my grandparents came from Europe. *This century.*"

Heather raised her open hands. "Sometimes you're guilty by association."

Sean considered this and concluded it was probably true, and there was not much he could do about it. Tessa's protective impulse had kicked in, and that's understandable. It's human nature. The truth was, he should have expected it. Anyway, they had exchanged apologies, so he was letting it go.

When he turned onto the library's street, Tessa's Volkswagen Bus came into view, parked in the same spot in front of the building.

He pushed in the headlight knob, darkening the roadway. Inside the VW, the silhouettes of three heads turned to watch him steer the Granada along the curb, tucking in behind the Bus.

When Sean pushed his door ajar, a strong breeze caught it, yanking it open. He stood, tilted his head back, and noticed how the sky had clouded over completely. The wind tore through the tree branch canopy, sending a squall of the first autumn leaves onto the street.

The entire group gathered beside the yellow and white Bus. "We should take the VW to the deadhouse," Tessa said in a low voice. "The back seat's been removed."

Sean shook his head. "If Grand-Bob sees a car he doesn't recognize, he might get suspicious."

A gust of wind blew, and they all shifted their stances, bracing against it.

Heather asked, "But wouldn't he be drunk by now?"

Sean shrugged. "Maybe. No, probably. But even so, it's less risky if we take my car. We can put the body in the back seat."

Tessa stared at the Granada. "Okay. We'll drop my grandparents off at the cemetery on the way."

She swung open the VW's side door and signaled for Sean to take a basket stowed behind the seat.

"Whoa," he said when he tried to lift it. He repositioned himself and hoisted it off the floor. "Is this filled with rocks?"

"I hope not," Norman said with a chuckle. "That's our feast."

Heather reached around to the front seat for her raincoat and shrugged it on.

"Good thinking," Tessa said. She handed her grandparents their jackets and pulled her own on while Norman helped Mildred into hers.

Tessa crawled inside and handed Heather a narrow wooden box. Then, she passed a drum to Norman. It appeared to be a small brass kettle with a buckskin stretched over the top, tied with rope, and a single carved wooden drumstick tucked into a loop in the cording. She crawled back out with a roll of heavy canvas and a short, handle-gripped shovel.

Sean led the way behind the Granada. He popped the trunk and pushed his scuba gear aside, clearing a space for the new cargo.

"Oh, wait," Heather said, sticking her index finger in the air. "We have something for the feast." She retrieved the doughnut box from the front seat and handed it to Tessa, who placed it inside the basket.

Sean pressed the trunk gently until it latched, without a slam. As he headed toward the front driver's door, he wondered where all the passengers would sit.

Heather promptly pulled open the front passenger door and slid across the bench seat to the center. She patted the passenger side of the seat and told Tessa, "You can sit up here."

Sean was pleased when Tessa didn't question the seating arrangement. She slid in beside Heather while Norman and Mildred climbed into the back.

When Sean started the car, Heather shot him a look. "I thought you fixed that muffler."

"I did," he said sheepishly. "The patch rusted out just recently." Sean regretted not thinking to repatch it. The extra noise would make sneaking around that much harder.

He kept the headlights off until they reached the next block. During the short drive, nobody spoke, and Sean wondered if the others shared his unease.

When the cemetery came into view, Sean pushed the headlight knob back in. He looked around for other cars. After convincing himself there were none, he turned into the entrance drive and followed it to his usual parking spot, where he shifted into park and cut the engine.

With no one uttering a word, all four doors swung open, and everyone climbed out. After Sean released the trunk, Tessa began passing out the items. "Let's put this stuff over there." She pointed to a spot beside the maintenance shack, under a roof overhang.

When all the items had been removed from the trunk, Tessa turned to Norman and Mildred. "Lie low in the darkness. We'll be back shortly." In no time, the elders disappeared into the shadows, like cats.

Back in the car, the three of them reverted to the front seat arrangement, causing Sean to wonder if Tessa was avoiding the rear seat or doing him a favor.

Silence stretched between them as Sean backed into the driveway. He felt so antsy that he could hardly enjoy sitting close to Heather. His tension skyrocketed as they circled through town, across the river, and onto the gravel road leading to Grand-Bob's house. Along the way, he lost his grip on the steering wheel and had to keep wiping his sweaty palms on his pant legs to regain it.

Sean killed the headlights as Grand-Bob's mobile home came into view. He coasted slowly from there, hoping to soften the sound of gravel crunching. Just past the house, the detached garage came into view, and, as they drew into the dead end, the shed attached to its side.

The deadhouse. What a creepy thing to call it, Sean thought.

After he turned off the ignition, they remained silent for a long moment, until Tessa whispered, "We need the lantern and the roll from the trunk."

Sean nodded, figuring his silhouette would at least be visible in the dark. When Tessa opened the door, the dome light came on. He turned to Heather. "Ready?"

She blinked and gave him a weak smile.

He returned the smile, probably just as weakly, and pushed open his door.

Grand-Bob's house was mostly dark, except for that familiar flickering light of the television, flashing in the narrow gap between the curtains.

Sean tiptoed to the trunk, turned the key slowly, and guided the lid up to prevent the noisy bounce. He grabbed his raincoat and slipped it on while Tessa retrieved the canvas roll. She signaled for

Sean to take the lantern, pushed the trunk lid down into a gentle latch, and set off for the deadhouse.

When they arrived at the entrance, Sean turned on the lantern and handed it to Heather. She tucked it against her body, behind the flap of her jacket, shading some of the brightness.

Sean recited *twelve, twenty-four, thirty-six* in his head as he dialed the numbers. He pulled on the lock, but it didn't release. A brief spark of panic flashed in his mind as he questioned whether the lock could have been replaced. *No way,* he reassured himself. *You probably forgot to go past the second digit.*

Sure enough, when he tried again, the lock clicked open. He exhaled in relief, then stepped aside. Tessa handed Heather the canvas roll and took the lantern.

Sean and Heather stood shoulder-to-shoulder, watching Tessa. She removed the lock, cracked the door ajar, and spoke something in her native tongue into the opening.

The wind blew, rattling a loose section of the garage's gutter.

Tessa pulled the door open further and nudged into the doorframe, extending the lantern into the interior. She leaned forward and peeked inside warily. After a long moment, she took another step and waved them in.

Sean motioned for Heather to go next. It was the polite thing to do, but he immediately regretted it, suspecting she would think cowardice was holding him back. She didn't hesitate, though.

Heather followed in the darkness of Tessa's shadow, with Sean close behind, his muscles as taut as rubber bands stretched to the limit. He caught a whiff of the lingering burnt sweetgrass odor mingled with cedar and a glimpse of the kayak against the wall.

Something brushed against his hand. He flinched away, only to realize it was Heather's fingers. He reached out and took her hand. Half of his tension melted away as their fingers intertwined.

Sean briefly wondered if Heather was holding his hand out of fear. Then he decided he would take it either way.

Tessa exhaled audibly. She stepped aside but kept the lantern held out. The room resolved into view, revealing Thomas lying on the bed of cedar boughs.

Dormant. Inert. Innocuous.

But is he really?

Sean riveted his gaze on the withered body as a vein throbbed in each temple. The shed clattered with a gust of wind.

"He hasn't moved," Heather whispered.

Sean nodded, looking over that shrunken apple face, appearing even ghastlier under the lantern light's shifting shadows. Heather was right, though: Thomas was just as they had left him.

She leaned into Sean. "This is surreal."

He squeezed her hand.

Tessa placed the lantern on the gravel floor and dropped to her knees beside Thomas's head, where she began unrolling the canvas. Heather released Sean's hand and crouched adjacent to Thomas's feet. Together, the women stretched out the canvas beside him.

Next, Tessa crawled near Thomas's head, signaling Sean to move toward his feet. Sean followed her direction and took hold of Thomas's ankles, wincing at the boniness of them. They lifted him off the floor and placed him on the canvas. Although Sean now knew what to expect, he was still unnerved by the awful lightness of the desiccated body. *Almost like Styrofoam,* he thought.

When Tessa began gathering the cedar boughs and packing them in the duffel bag, Heather and Sean jumped in to help. Tessa held back the last bough, draping it over Thomas's torso.

With the cedar cleared from the floor, Tessa passed Heather the duffel bag and the lantern and returned to Thomas's head, grasping one corner of the canvas in each hand. Sean took the other end, and they raised him off the gravel.

Heather stepped clear as Sean swung sideways. He walked backward toward the door, slowing to maneuver through the doorframe.

After Tessa exited the deadhouse, they shifted to carry him sideways. Heather locked the door behind them and then switched off the lantern, plunging them into blackness.

As they headed toward the car, the wind blew the bough off Thomas, exposing the turtle shell necklace. Heather plucked the cedar branch from the ground and placed it back on Thomas, then hurried ahead, pulling open the rear car door.

Tessa ducked and lowered herself onto the seat, resting Thomas's head and shoulders on her lap. Sean shuddered. She scooted across the seat until she reached the opposite end.

When Sean saw how Thomas's feet extended beyond the car's width, he attempted to push them in. The broken hip leg hinged unnaturally, but the other remained locked. Sean angled in and lifted from underneath the good knee, folding it in. He arranged both feet on the seat, and when Tessa gave him a thumbs-up, he guided the door closed, pressing until it latched.

Facing him in the darkness, Heather let out a long, sighing breath.

Sean reached for her hand. She took hold and pulled him toward her, wrapping her free arm around him and drawing him into an embrace. As Sean zeroed in on the warmth of her body and the sensation of her hair whipping in the breeze against his cheek, Heather spoke softly into his ear, "That was the easy part."

A brief spray of raindrops hit the windshield as they drove across the bridge toward town. Sean activated his wipers, but nobody mentioned the rain. Although it lasted only a few seconds, it served as a threat of what might lie ahead.

A pair of headlights bore down on them from the opposite direction. As Sean got nearer, he caught sight of a light bar on the other car's roof. He immediately lifted his foot off the gas pedal. "Damn, it's a sheriff's car."

"Were you speeding?" Heather asked.

Sean looked at his speedometer. He was going 45. But he'd been too preoccupied to even think about the speed limit, so if there had been a sign along that stretch, he'd missed it. "I don't even know what the speed limit is here."

With his heart jackhammering in his chest, Sean eyed the car's taillights in his rearview mirror, waiting to see if the brake lights would illuminate.

What would he do if they came on? Although he'd heard nothing from the sheriff since the interview, that didn't mean he was no longer under suspicion. And with a cadaver in the back seat...

As the seconds ticked by, the car receded in the mirror. Sean started to relax. When he turned off the state highway into the village, he finally breathed a full sigh of relief.

The riverside road darkened as it transitioned from the residential zone to the cemetery. Without turning around, Heather asked, "You okay, Tessa?"

"We're fine."

Heather didn't respond, leaving Sean to ponder how Tessa had said "we're" instead of "I'm." Did that mean she knew how Thomas felt? Or was she merely saying he was...what was the term she'd used earlier? *Tranquil.* There was no telling.

Before entering the graveyard, Sean looked around to confirm no cars were coming. He killed the headlights, turned in, and switched off the ignition as soon as he parked.

Two shadows emerged from behind the maintenance shack, sending Sean into a brief panic, until the outline of the drum gave Norman away. The elders lingered beside the building while Sean climbed out and pulled open the rear door.

Tessa waited as Sean extended Thomas's legs and took hold of the canvas. They gradually maneuvered him out of the car, with Tessa steadily working her way across the seat.

After Tessa stood, they carried him around the car and over to the burial place. "Put him down over here," Mildred said, pointing at a spot on the ground just outside the border chain, at the point furthest from the driveway.

Sean and Tessa lowered Thomas onto the grass. Norman and Mildred moved over to stand sentry on either side of him, while Tessa beckoned Sean and Heather away. They followed her back toward the Granada, where they huddled. "We'll prepare for the ceremony while you take the car back to the library." She pointed at the clearing in front of the log mission house. "When you get back, you can watch from over there."

Heather gave the okay sign, grabbed Sean's arm, and pulled him toward the car.

Chapter 24

As they drove out of the cemetery, Sean asked, "So, why does she want us to keep a distance?"

"Only natives can participate in the burial," Heather said. "We'll be included in the pipe ceremony and the feast, though."

Sean mulled this over. Would the presence of a white person mess up the ceremony? Or was this some sort of secret the natives didn't want white people to know about? Or was it something else altogether? He contemplated asking Heather.

"The streets are deserted."

The sound of Heather's words snapped Sean back into the moment. He looked around. It was true. Although it wasn't even nine o'clock, no cars or people were in sight. With a shrug, he said, "Maybe people are hiding from the coming storm."

One block before turning onto the library's street, the first sign of life appeared. They passed Felix the German shepherd, sniffing a fire hydrant, his owner standing patiently at the other end of the leash. When the man waved, Sean returned it, hoping the guy wasn't getting suspicious about these non-townies.

He coasted up behind the Volkswagen, grimacing at the noise from his leaking muffler. As soon as he could, he killed the ignition.

Heather swung open her door and slipped out, while Sean fetched a baseball cap from the glove box and wedged it over his head.

Thunder rumbled in the distance as he closed his door gently, latching it without a slam.

Since Heather had set off without waiting, Sean had to hurry to catch up. A gust of wind that almost tore off his hat carried a wave of loose leaves down the street toward them.

"You're a speedy walker," he said when he closed in on her.

"Don't be a lollygagger," she said with a forced grin.

They walked side-by-side while Sean tried to work up the guts to reach for her hand. When he eventually made his move, she promptly intertwined her fingers between his. He tried to contain his elation and act like he was used to this sort of thing.

Thunder sounded again, closer this time.

The last row of houses loomed a block ahead, backdropped by darkness...the graveyard.

Heather pointed down the street at a boarded-up house with charred patches covering portions of the upper sections. Sean immediately understood this was the house Thomas had set ablaze, killing two people. The dreadful sight of it ruined his mood and drove home the importance of their plan. Thomas *must* be stopped.

Straight ahead, the pathway between two houses disappeared into the gloom. They walked silently toward it, moving slowly to allow their eyes to adjust to the darkness. As the sidewalk narrowed, the enclosing tree branches swayed in the wind, like arms reaching for them.

When the path opened and the first headstones appeared, lightning flashed, and thunder cracked, louder this time. They stopped and exchanged a nervous glance, but neither spoke.

Before venturing forward, they scanned their surroundings to get their bearings. "Over there," Sean said when he spotted the shadows of the small building cluster across the grounds. Heather promptly took off in that direction, towing him along.

As they picked their way through the graveyard, lightning flashed again, illuminating the sea of headstones surrounding them, like countless fingers reaching up from the ground.

Shortly after the ensuing crack of thunder faded, Heather halted. "Hear that?"

Sean cocked an ear and listened, but heard nothing. He shook his head.

She whispered, "Are you deaf?"

"Well, I *have* gone to a lot of rock concerts."

She chuckled timidly. "I hear drumming." She gave him a forward tug, and they continued their trek.

Before long, Sean picked up the sound of the drumming: a slow, steady cadence. He narrowed his eyes and stared toward where they were heading. Moving shadows around the burial place began taking shape.

Their pace slowed as they approached the log mission house. Sean examined the scene, now no more than thirty yards off. Tessa was digging in the center of the burial site. Norman remained standing near Thomas, tapping the drum lightly, like making every effort to keep the volume low. Mildred trod around the burial circle, slowly waving a bundle of smoking sweetgrass, singing a prayer in her native tongue.

Sean followed Heather as she led the way forward, stopping beside the massive obelisk that had been erected for the massacre victims.

They took a position near the base of the memorial marker and watched from twenty yards away. Within a minute, raindrops began falling. Heather stretched her raincoat's hood over her head. The cold water and the gusting wind prickled Sean's skin, so he, too, pulled his hood over his baseball cap. Within seconds, the other three paused to do the same.

The glass lantern swayed in the wind, but somehow, the candle remained lit, casting a weak shimmer over the setting.

Under the pelting rain, Tessa went back to her frantic digging. She had already reached a depth of a foot or more, but Sean noticed her gasping for breath. How long could she keep up her pace? He desperately wanted to help but held back, knowing he must remain an observer.

When the rain grew heavier, Heather leaned against him, and he wrapped his arm around her. Lightning flashed, and thunder crashed a fraction of a second later.

Norman hunched his shoulders and turned against the direction of the driving shower. Mildred huddled over the smoking bundle, like attempting to keep it dry.

The rain increased to a downpour, drowning out the drumbeat and the singing. Sean and Heather dashed to the mission house and took shelter beneath the little overhang covering the door. But despite the deluge, Tessa, Mildred, and Norman remained on task.

A tremendous lightning flash lit the world in a blaze of light—only it wasn't white; it was purple. And this time, no thunder followed.

The bright purple glare lingered, diminishing slowly into normal daylight. The rain was gone.

When the scene came back into view, Sean's mouth fell open.

Heather peeled away from under Sean's arm and swung around with wide eyes.

The sun shone brightly in the clear blue sky.

Sean turned one way, then the other, straining to make sense of their new surroundings.

The mission house remained directly behind him, but the obelisk was gone. Almost a dozen small log buildings stood in a line, just beyond the open lot where the obelisk had stood. In the area where the burial place had been, a split-rail fence surrounded a pen of hogs.

Outside one building, a woman and two girls husked corn. They were dark-complected, wearing old-fashioned colonial-style clothing.

Two boys ran past, chasing a dog.

A fruit tree orchard stretched behind the row of log buildings, where the cemetery should have been. Sean recognized both apple and cherry trees amongst the grove.

A woman was stringing fish to dry between two of the log structures. A boy came into the clearing from the direction of the river, carrying more fish and wearing...

Sean blinked.

Around the boy's neck hung a turtle shell necklace.

Heather turned to Sean with an expression of bewilderment. "What is this?"

Before he could respond, another brilliant flash of lightning cleared the scene, but what replaced it was a visage of horror.

Bodies were piled where the obelisk should have been, their heads bloodied. Outside the closest building lay another mass of corpses.

A gathering of scruffy men clamored beyond the now-empty hog pen, dressed in ragged colonial clothing, whooping, and passing drinks.

Heather gasped. She pointed behind the nearby building, where a boy crawled out of an opening in the foundation. Sean glimpsed a turtle shell swinging from the boy's neck as he rose to his feet. He turned and stumbled away, revealing a gory open wound covering the top and back of his head.

A third flash of lightning yielded another scene altogether. The buildings were all gone, replaced with piles of charcoal. Sean and Heather turned around to find a heap of ash where the mission house had stood. Two gray-haired men sifted through the rubble. One pulled an ash-darkened bone from the ruins and tossed it into a nearby stack they'd accumulated.

A boy watched from the clearing, weeping, a turtle shell hanging from his neck. Behind him, a hole had been opened in the ground, in the location of the burial place.

Another bolt of lightning flashed, the most powerful yet, but this time, a clap of thunder followed as the light transitioned into purple, then cleared, leaving darkness in its place.

The modern-day scene came back into view, including Tessa and her grandparents. It was raining once again, although lighter than before.

Heather turned to Sean with wide eyes. "It's like we saw flashes from the past, but now we're back."

Too dazed to respond, he just nodded.

The hole Tessa continued digging was now at least two feet deep, but each additional shovelful looked like watery mud.

Mildred was still praying, but her sweetgrass bundle was now steaming more than smoking.

Carrying on with his steady drumbeat, Norman abruptly stopped and shot a downward look.

When Sean followed Norman's gape, his heart seized as panic erupted in his mind.

Thomas had rolled over. He was grasping Norman, one hand manacled onto each ankle. Using his one good leg, he levered himself into a forward lunge, wrapping his arms around Norman's calves and dropping him in a tackle.

Sean took a step forward, but Heather grabbed his shoulders and yelled, "We can't interfere!"

He wriggled free from her grip and stumbled toward the others.

Tessa saw him coming and held up her hand in a halt sign. "Stay back!"

It took everything in him to obey Tessa's command. *Don't screw this up,* he told himself, stalling. *They know what they're doing. You don't.* He stood there helplessly while Heather stepped forward and leaned against him.

Tessa threw down the shovel and hurdled over the chain, falling to her knees beside Thomas. Mildred moved over to his opposite flank. They placed their hands on Thomas's upper back. His body jolted, then went stiff as they spoke to him in Lunaapeew.

Lightning flashed, but not as bright, and the thunder that followed sounded more distant.

Thomas gradually went limp. Norman scooted out from underneath him, climbed onto his feet, and picked up the drum. He began beating it once again.

Sean put his open hand out to gauge the intensity of the rainfall. The storm was passing.

Tessa went back to the mound and resumed digging.

Mildred pushed herself onto her feet, leaving Thomas on the ground. He remained still. She picked up the sweetgrass bundle and set about attempting to relight it. Before long, a faint yellow glow emerged, and a tendril of smoke rose into the air. She held the smudge stick upside-down, allowing the heat to dry itself out, and soon, the flames grew. After blowing out the blaze, she began slowly waving the smoking bundle above Thomas and resumed singing prayers in her native language.

The rain diminished further, with each rumble of thunder becoming progressively quieter.

Before long, the sweetgrass bundle had burned to a stub. Mildred held it over the chain and shook it, spreading embers over the mound. With her hand empty, her praying diminished to a whisper before falling silent. Norman's drumming softened, then went still. Tessa climbed out of the hole and bowed her head.

"It stopped raining," Heather whispered.

Sean tilted his head back to clear the bill of his cap, but felt no drops on his face.

Tessa, Mildred, and Norman remained frozen for a handful of minutes. Eventually, Tessa stepped off the mound and over the chain. She retrieved the cedar bough that had been draped over Thomas and placed it in the hole.

Norman put down the drum. All three encircled Thomas, crouched, and shifted him back onto the canvas. Norman and Tessa each took an end and lifted him over the chain and up the mass grave's slope. They lowered him onto a spot near the center of the mound, just above the freshly dug hole.

The trio dropped to their knees behind Thomas. They placed their hands on him and rolled him into the hole, where he settled face up.

A faint rumble sounded. When it didn't fade away like thunder would, Heather gave Sean a questioning look.

Sean shrugged, feeling the earth tremble in sync with the rumble. As the seconds ticked by, the tremor strengthened while the sound grew in volume. This wasn't like an earthquake, though. It was more like a steady thrum reverberating through the ground.

An energy.

Heather and Sean leaned against one another for stability. The burial site's candle lantern jiggled on its pole.

Still kneeling behind the new grave, the three others raised their arms, palms open, and tilted their heads back. Tessa cried out in Lunaapeew.

Movement in the hole caught Sean's eye, and he went rigid in alarm. He was just about to call out to warn them, but he stalled. He squinted, trying to decipher what he was witnessing. From a distance, with the darkness, he couldn't sort out the sight. All he could tell now was that it wasn't Thomas moving. It was more like...

"Oh, my God," Heather said, interrupting Sean's thoughts. "Earthworms."

Sean blinked and refocused his eyes. He cringed. "You're right...he's covered in them!"

Dumbstruck, Sean watched the writhing layer thicken and swell. Before long, Thomas's shape was no longer discernible. All that was visible was a squirming mass filling the hole. But then, the wormy shape began to contract. It sank like a steadily deflating air mattress.

As the wriggling heap of worms shrank, white objects took their place, protruding up from the bottom of the dark hole.

"That's his skeleton," Heather gasped, beating Sean to the realization. She gawked at the sight with her jaw hanging open.

When he recognized the shape of the skull and ribcage, Sean covered his mouth with an open palm.

Before long, the last of the worms had receded from view. Simultaneously, the rumble tapered off, and the ground grew still.

Tessa fell silent, and all three dropped their arms. A faint, purple glow formed around the skeleton, casting an eerie gleam on their faces. The illumination gathered in a cloud and began to rise. It hovered above the hole, then spread across the burial site, where it hung for a spell. The aureole expanded and thinned while rising into the sky, where it dimmed before fading away completely.

Norman turned toward the two women, who slumped as if exhausted. Nobody moved. Eventually, Mildred pulled a handkerchief out of her pocket and dabbed it underneath Tessa's nose.

"Her nose was bleeding," Heather whispered.

Sean nodded while holding his stare.

Tessa rose slowly to her feet. She stepped over the grave, crouched, and reached into it with both hands. She began stirring the contents, like mixing up the bones so they would retain none of their functional arrangement. Then she plucked something from the hole and slid it into her pocket. She pushed upright, picked up the spade, and began shoveling the wet soil into the hole, gradually covering the skeleton.

They all watched in silence as Tessa filled the grave. When she was done, she pieced together the patches of sod, until the covered hole blended in with the rest of the site.

While Norman helped Mildred to her feet, Tessa wiped her hands clean on the wet grass.

Mildred wandered down to the chain at the spot closest to Sean and Heather, lifted her head, and waved for them to come.

EPILOGUE

SEAN AND HEATHER STOOD between the others, outside the chain encircling the burial site. Following Mildred's lead, they each sprinkled the handful of dried tobacco leaves Norman had given them over the grassy mound.

When Sean bowed his head, the nearby stone epitaph embedded in the ground drew his gaze. The hanging candle cast just enough faint light to reveal the carved words that had already been permanently etched into his mind:

BURIAL SITE OF INDIAN MARTYRS 1782

A hollow ache twisted in his gut as he reflected on the people who were buried there and the atrocity of their destruction.

Norman stepped aside first. While he retrieved the pipe from the wooden box, Mildred and Tessa turned away, gesturing for Sean and Heather to gather in a nearby circle.

Nobody spoke as Norman lit the pipe. He stoked the burning tobacco with a few puffs, and Sean noticed how good it smelled—even better than cigarettes, which still appealed to him over a year after quitting.

"Ordinarily, we would sit for this," Norman said, frowning at the soggy ground. He turned, pulled a heavy draw through the pipe, and blew out a steady billow into the air, now still since the storm had passed. He waited for a spell, pivoted ninety degrees, and blew another stream of smoke.

"We start facing north," Mildred explained. "Then east, then south, and finally, west."

Sean nodded, feeling honored by the opportunity to participate in the pipe ceremony. He knew little of their culture, but these were good people, and he would be eternally grateful for what they'd done.

When Norman finished, he passed the pipe to Mildred.

"Our elders go first," Tessa said.

As Mildred followed the same routine, nobody spoke. Sean considered how no one had mentioned anything about what had just happened, yet somehow, this seemed natural. The five of them had shared a mystical experience. Even what he and Heather had experienced—glimpses into the past—needed no discussion or explanation.

Tessa smoked next, and when she was done, she handed the pipe to Sean.

He took a moment to look it over. The long-stemmed pipe was fashioned from stone. He ran his fingers over the carvings on the side of the bowl: a bear on one side, a beaver on the other.

Sean put the pipe to his lips and sucked through it. He held the richly flavored smoke in his mouth without inhaling, turned to face in the same direction as the others had, and blew it out.

When he finished his fourth drag, he passed the pipe to Heather. She looked at it uncertainly, took a puff, and immediately launched into a coughing fit.

Everyone laughed. Once she recovered, Heather said, "Please don't tell my dad I smoked," triggering a fresh round of uncontrolled laughter—one of those collective fits of slaphappy delirium people sometimes fall into after they've made it through an exhausting, stressful situation.

When their serious moods were restored, Heather resumed the ceremony. By the way she puffed, Sean could tell she was being extra careful not to inhale any smoke.

After her fourth turn, Norman took the pipe. He knocked the ashes out and replaced the pipe in the box. When he stood, he gave a wide smile and declared, "It's time for the feast."

They gathered around a picnic bench beside the burial site, in front of the maintenance shack. Tessa dug a towel out of the basket and began wiping down the seats.

The clouds had cleared enough for the gibbous moon to make an appearance, bathing their surroundings with moonlight. Sean circled the building, surveying the area. Upon returning, he said, "If we move to the other side of the shack, we'd be better hidden."

"That's a good idea," Tessa said, taking hold of the bench.

Heather nudged her over and squeezed in beside her, while Sean took the other end. They lifted the table a few inches off the ground and hauled it to the concealed spot he had in mind.

Under the lantern's light, Tessa and Mildred went to work arranging the food, dishing most of it onto five plates. Each got a serving of some type of meat, a thick piece of cornbread, and a generous spoonful of cucumber and tomato salad. On three other plates, they arranged a small portion of each dish.

Heather opened the doughnut box and tilted it so they could see inside. "Do you like apple fritters?"

Tessa, Norman, and Mildred took turns peering in, but each shrugged.

"You're in for a treat. Sean turned me on to these things."

They added one fritter to each of the five plates, divided the sixth, and added a piece to each of the three other plates.

Tessa pulled a half gallon of apple cider from the bottom of the basket. "I've never had an apple fritter before, but I imagine this will go well with them." She poured some into each of five cups, then dribbled a few drops onto the three other plates.

"Sorry the soup's cold," Mildred said as Tessa removed a covered pot from the basket.

"Well, we can't exactly have a fire in the graveyard," Heather said, glancing at Sean with a smile.

"I'm sure it will be tasty," Sean said. Part of him was being polite, but as hungry as he was, another part truly believed it.

Mildred began spooning it out into five small bowls. "Corn soup is just as good cold as it is hot." When finished, she drizzled a bit onto each of the three extra plates.

Just then, Sean noticed Norman leering at his cap. Norman pointed at it. "What is that?"

Sean took it off and looked at it, incredulous. "You don't know Chief Wahoo?" He held it out for Norman to get a better look.

Norman's face hardened.

Sean was getting ready to explain how this was the logo of the Cleveland Indians until it dawned on him that Norman already knew very well. Sean's cheeks heated up. He stared at the logo he had always thought was cool, finding himself in a precarious position. In the presence of his new friends—the people who would never get a medal for the heroic act they'd just performed—he saw for the first time an almost wicked-looking racial caricature. He briefly wondered if he should claim the team was honoring Indians with their name and the logo. Although he had heard people say this, it suddenly seemed more like a justification overreach than anything.

He took a few steps, pulled the raccoon-proof trash bin open, and tossed the cap inside.

Norman's stern look melted away. He smiled and patted Sean on the shoulder.

Tessa picked up one of the three plates. The elders motioned for Sean and Heather to follow as Tessa led the way to the burial place. She stepped over the chain and carried it up the slope.

As Tessa set the plate over the spot where Thomas had been buried, Mildred turned to face Sean and Heather. "She's leaving a plate for Thomas's spirit. For his journey, to meet his creator."

After Tessa stepped back over the chain, the group returned to the picnic table. But instead of sitting, Tessa picked up the two other plates and headed toward the river.

The elders tagged behind Tessa, beckoning the teenagers to follow. As they set off, Sean looked at Heather questioningly. She responded with a subtle shrug.

The group crossed the roadway and drew in on the stone wall. Tessa placed both plates on top.

Mildred looked at Sean. "One is for your friend Karl." She turned to Heather. "The other is for your mother Marilyn."

Sean's throat tightened. He stared across the river, blinking away the sting in his eyes. When Heather sniffed, he wrapped his arm around her and pulled her in. She leaned against his shoulder and faced the river.

"Thank you," Sean said, his voice cracking.

Heather sucked in a quivering breath and nodded emphatically.

Mildred pulled both of them into an embrace. When Sean realized Tessa and Norman were joining the group hug, a tear spilled out from each of his eyes.

After a while, Mildred let go to speak. "All that's happened...Karl, Marilyn..." She hesitated, then tossed her head in the direction of the cemetery. "...our ancestors...we've lost loved ones, friends, and family. All innocent." She bowed her head and paused. After a while, she removed her handkerchief and wiped tears from her cheeks. "We can't undo these wrongs. But after tonight, we can find solace knowing there won't be any more. Not here, at least."

The group fell into a long, solemn lull until Norman cleared his throat. "Our feast is getting cold."

Tessa broke into a grin. "I'm not sure about that, but it *is* time." She turned and headed off toward the picnic bench.

Sean and Heather followed hand in hand, their shoulders bumping along the way. Once there, they stood at the end of the table, waiting for the others to take their seats. They settled next to one another, beside Tessa, and across from the elders.

The rest of the clouds had cleared out, providing ample moonlight for the feast. The temperature had dropped, giving the night air that hint of early autumn. Sean and Heather pressed tightly against each other.

Sean started with the corn soup. After enjoying a few spoonfuls, he said, "You were right, Mildred. The soup's delicious, even cold."

Mildred held up her half-eaten apple fritter. "This is, too."

"Ahhh!" Heather feigned outrage. "You're supposed to save that for dessert."

Everyone laughed.

As he scraped his bowl with the spoon to get every last bit, Sean watched Heather take tentative nibbles of the meat. She furrowed her brow and chewed slowly, studying what was left on her fork. "Is this chicken?"

"Rabbit," Tessa said, then took a bite of her cornbread.

Heather froze, and her eyes grew wide.

Sean tried to hold his response, but he let out a stifled chortle.

Heather gave a dramatic scowl. "I'm eating Thumper?"

Everyone laughed. Heather exaggerated her grimace.

"Think of it as Bugs Bunny," Sean said. "He can be pretty annoying."

Heather promptly chomped down on the rest, triggering another round of belly laughs.

When the laughter died off, Mildred said something to Norman in their native language. Tessa saw Sean and Heather exchange a curious glance, so she leaned over and put an open palm against her mouth, pretending to speak privately. "She said you make a good couple."

Sean felt his cheeks catch fire. With no idea how to respond, he avoided eye contact with all of them. He wasn't even sure if they *were* a couple. Were they?

Heather stroked the hair on the back of his head. "We do, don't we?"

When Sean turned to face her, she was smiling at the elders. Without warning, she turned and kissed him on the lips.

In the shock of the moment, he thought, *Well, there's your answer, dumb-ass.*

Tessa and Mildred responded with a duet of, "Awww..."

When Heather pulled away, Sean fell into a bashful smile. Feeling everyone's eyes on him, he fixed his own gaze on his plate and waited desperately for the moment to pass.

It was Heather who saved him. "Look!" She pointed in the direction of the river.

Everyone turned to look that way. At first, Sean couldn't tell what she was pointing at, but just as he opened his mouth to ask, he noticed two faint purple glows wafting above the river, near where they had left the plates. Then, it hit him: the plates weren't there anymore.

He scanned the area, figuring a breeze had blown them off the wall. There was no sign of them, though. Anyway, the air had been still since the storm had passed, so they couldn't have blown away. They were simply gone. The luminescent clouds faded as they rose and soon disappeared entirely.

Sean waited for someone to say something, but nobody did. The elders rotated back around and all three resumed eating without ever showing the slightest reaction. Whatever had happened, they took it in stride. When Sean ticked his eyes at Heather, she merely gave him a wide-eyed stare, her fingers clasping her heart-shaped locket.

"Oh," Tessa said, "I almost forgot..." She leaned back, reached into her pocket, and placed something on the table beside Sean. "We think *you* should have this."

Sean recoiled. His mouth suddenly felt dry as he regarded the small turtle shell that had hung from Thomas's neck. His first reaction was to hurl it into the river, but part of him didn't even want to touch it. *Is this some sort of joke?* he wondered, but the earnest expression on Tessa's face told him otherwise.

"Turtles are sacred creatures in native cultures," Norman said.

Dozens of thoughts streamed through Sean's head. Did he want this thing?

"The turtle represents wisdom, health, protection, and fertility," Mildred added.

With a hard swallow, Sean forced himself to touch it. Picking it up in one hand, he rubbed his thumb over the smooth surface, working to gather his thoughts.

He cleared his throat. "Everything that's happened...it's so much to take in." He stared at the turtle shell and chewed on his lower lip. "I lost my best friend. Heather lost her mother. But our losses brought us together, and now we have each other."

Heather wrapped her arm around him and leaned in.

"We discovered this hidden threat." He looked over his shoulder at the burial site and noticed Thomas's plate was gone too. Dipping his head, he added, "Like fallout from that horrible event all these years later."

He turned to Tessa and her grandparents. "Fortunately, Heather was smart enough to reach out to you. Nobody else would have believed it. But thank God, *you* listened. *You* were willing to help."

"For sure," Heather interjected. "I don't know what we would have done without you."

Tessa responded with a faint smile.

Sean took a deep breath. "By teaming up, we did something incredible. Others would have died, but not now."

He paused, pursed his lips, and returned his gaze to his plate. "In the process, we made new friends and learned a little about your amazing culture." He felt himself choking up.

Heather squeezed him and nodded her agreement.

"Taking the good with the bad, I feel lucky for all this." Sean's eyes went watery. He blinked, and a tear spilled down his cheek. He wiped it away on his sleeve. "It's a big part of who I am now. It always will be."

Grasping the turtle shell in both hands, he held it up. "This is like a token of everything that has happened, so I'm honored to have it." He turned his eyes to Tessa, Norman, and then Mildred. "Thank you to each of you."

Sean Davidson turned to Heather and said nothing, but simply gave her the kiss he'd been holding onto for so very long.

AFTERWORD

YEARS AGO, I READ a nonfiction, historical book by Allan Eckert entitled *That Dark and Bloody River: Chronicles of the Ohio River Valley*. One event covered in the book was the massacre of 96 peaceful Native Americans in 1782 in a Moravian missionary village named Gnadenhutten (these days pronounced locally as Juh-Nay-Den-Huh-Tin), in what was then considered the western frontier, the Northwest Territory. Today, Gnadenhutten is a village in Tuscarawas County, Ohio. Locals often shorten the village name to "Gnaden" (Juh-Nay-Den).

Learning about this atrocity shocked me. Not only was the incident cruel beyond comprehension, but I couldn't fathom why I had never learned of it, despite growing up in Ohio. How could our society lack awareness of such a thing?

So, real-life events inspired this book, including the unlikely story of Thomas, a teenage boy who somehow survived being clubbed and scalped, escaping to tell others what happened. For the remainder of his short life, Thomas endured great suffering from his head injuries. Although he was known to be an excellent swimmer, a seizure while fishing led to his death by drowning.

I hope that, in some small way, sharing this tale will help raise awareness of the tragic incident it is built upon.

Although I write about ghosts and I'm intrigued by the idea of them, I can't say I've ever seen one. But if ever there was a place where ghosts could be felt, it's at the Gnadenhutten massacre burial site, a stone's throw from the Tuscarawas River, surrounded by an expansive cemetery.

If you're in the area, I would encourage you to visit. The onsite museum operates under limited hours that vary seasonally, so be sure to check the hours in advance (I'm speaking from experience here!).

I mostly depicted the area as it exists in real life, however, I took some liberties to suit my made-up story. It's a fiction writer's prerogative, after all. Those familiar with the area will easily spot my alterations.

I strove to portray the culture of the massacre victims' descendants authentically, within the limits of my outsider's perspective, and with the understanding that native cultures vary widely. I hope those with an insider's perspective will forgive me for where I fell short.

If you're interested in learning more about the Gnadenhutten massacre, you may want to start with the movies on YouTube (at least, they're available as I write this). The Eckert book I mentioned above provides a detailed account of the event, although it constitutes only a relatively small part of a much broader historical narrative. In the more recent book *Anatomy of a Massacre: The Destruction of Gnadenhutten, 1782*, Eric Sterner provides a comprehensive assessment of the history leading up to the event and the many factors that culminated in the massacre. Sterner does an excellent job of recounting the indiscriminate brutality of that era, and he characterizes the uncertainty behind many widespread beliefs about the event and what led up to it.

The books I have published are all set in Homer County, Ohio, a fictionalized county fashioned in my imagination from areas of Coshocton, Holmes, and Tuscarawas Counties, which I regularly visit. I feel drawn to this beautiful region in the Ohio countryside, although I also wonder: am I alone in feeling it conceals a lonesome and haunting presence?

Acknowledgments

Although Atrocity is a work of fiction, and Moravian Village and Homer County, Ohio, are fictionalized places, they are inspired by actual events in what is now Gnadenhutten, Tuscarawas County, Ohio. As a result, I felt the need to represent the events and the place with a certain degree of authenticity while applying some creative license.

I want to acknowledge the countless people who have worked to memorialize the Gnadenhutten massacre, including historians, generations of Gnadenhutten Historical Society members, and the Native Americans who have sought to preserve the memory of what happened.

Because the massacre was an actual event affecting indigenous people, I felt the story should include native characters at its center. My problem was that I didn't feel equipped to do this without help.

Andy McMillen, President of the Gnadenhutten Historical Society, assisted me by introducing me to Theresa Johnson of The Delaware Nation at Moraviantown, Ontario, Canada. This community is one of the Delaware (Lenape, or Lunaapeew) bands, which they believe settled in the area after the Gnadenhutten massacre. You can learn more about the community at:

https://delawarenation.on.ca/

I had written most of the story before I connected with Theresa, but I had stalled and didn't know how to end it. It was almost as though Theresa knew what I needed to complete the story, because everything fell into place after we spoke. She graciously shared some of the traditional ceremonial practices from her community's culture, which I weaved into this story with a dose of my own embellishments. Along the way, as you might have guessed, Theresa and her grandmother became inspirations for characters.

While the Gnadenhutten massacre victims are usually identified as Delaware Indians, Theresa believes many came from other tribes. Native cultures and their practices vary widely, but I hope I was able to tell a culturally sensitive story with an authentic feel. If I managed to achieve this, I have Theresa to thank.

My son-in-law, Nick Bryan, assisted me as a subject matter expert. An avid fisherman with a background in biology, he is the most knowledgeable amateur naturalist I know. He advised and fact-checked me on river biology, scuba diving, and environmental river surveys.

I appreciate the help of my Ohio horror writing colleague, DM Guay, who has a background in journalism. She crafted a newspaper article I included in this book, which appears far more genuine than I could have done alone. DM has also helped me by hosting regular "author business meetings," teaching me the business side of author life.

Thanks to my friends John Henry, Scott Dwyer, Billy Halpin, and John McCloskey, who served as beta readers on my first draft of this story. Their feedback and suggestions helped me see the forest beyond the trees, guiding my first revision rounds. My wife, Mary, also helped as a beta reader, but her never-ending support extends miles beyond that.

I appreciate the contributions from my monthly critique workshop colleagues, Kelly Griffiths, Sean Seebach, Rami Ungar, Ann Heyward, Randall Drum, and Jonathan Mitchell. The members of this group each reviewed portions of this story. I've learned so much from these sessions and love our camaraderie!

My critique partners Sean Seebach, Kelly Griffiths, and Ann Heyward dedicated significant time to reviewing and editing the entire manuscript. I can't tell you how many times I've read their markups and thought, *Of course! Why didn't I see that?*

Special thanks to Kelly for her extra-critical eye and extra-thoughtful suggestions. The story's last sentence is hers, word for word. It's much better than what I had written.

As you can see, I relied heavily on others to complete this book. If you liked it, I need to share the credit, because, truth be told, some of my best ideas don't come from me.

As I neared completion of the manuscript, I met Theresa Johnson in person at the Day of Remembrance Ceremony on March 8, 2025. This annual commemorative event for the victims of the Gnadenhutten massacre is held on the anniversary of the tragedy, and Theresa has organized it in recent years. It's hard to describe the moving experience of seeing so many Native people, most of whom had traveled long distances across the US and Canada, gathering to remember what had happened and memorialize their lost ancestors.

Anushiik (thank you) to Theresa for reviewing the near-final manuscript for cultural sensitivity. Considering her familiarity with the massacre (including Thomas's role), her enthusiasm for my story, and her appreciation of how it might help increase awareness of the tragedy encouraged me as I prepared for publication.

Anushiik (thank you) to Kamryn Whiteye, Takwaxkwe of Eelünaapéewi Lahkéewiit (Lenape, Delaware Nation), for permitting me to include her poignant speech at the 2025 Day of Remembrance Ceremony in the section that follows. Anushiik also to Kamryn for taking the time to read the final version. I truly appreciated her positive feedback and the word choice suggestions she made to align with Native culture.

Through the support of Theresa and Kamryn, this story centers on the Delaware Nation at Moraviantown community (Eelünaapéewi Lahkéewiit) in Ontario, Canada. However, there are other Lenape (Delaware) tribes and communities throughout what is now considered the US and Canada who identify as descendants of the massacre victims, including: Munsee-Delaware Nation, Muncey, Ontario; Delawares of the Six Nations of the Grand River; Delaware Nation of Anadarko, Oklahoma; Delaware Tribe of Indians of Bartlesville, Oklahoma; Stockbridge-Munsee of Bowler, Wisconsin; and The Munsee Tribe in Kansas. This story is a tribute to all of them.

Finally, I would like to thank my readers. Knowing someone has taken the time to read and enjoy one of my books gives me great joy. I've heard that some readers never read the Acknowledgments section, so if you're one of them, I feel bad that I don't have a way of expressing my appreciation. But if you're still with me, THANK YOU!

Lenape Resiliency and the Gnadenhutten Massacre

March 8, 2025 Day of Remembrance Speech

By Kamryn Whiteye, Takwaxkwe of Eelünaapéewi Lahkéewiit (Lenape, Delaware Nation)[1]

Kwiingu-neewulohmwa, nii ndushiinzii Kamryn, was nii ndushiinzii Takwaxkwe, nii noonjiiyayi Eelünaapéewi Lahkéewiit.

Good morning everyone, my name is Kamryn Whiteye, it is also Turtle Woman. I am from Delaware Nation, and I am a Delaware woman.

I am up here today because I was driving down with my dad George — he is over there taking a video of me — and I had the urge to speak to the youth, the young people that are here today.

In my community of Eelünaapéewi Lahkéewiit, from a youth, I was running youth events. I had the urge to do that because I knew what it was like growing up on-reserve, and I had my own

1. Reprinted with permission.

struggles. I wanted the youth to know that they were safe and they were supported, and they had peers that knew what they were going through. I have some dancing protégés here, Lola and Harper. I am back in the community — I have been away for a few years at university — I am really glad to be here with you all today.

I am so proud of every single one of our community members here today, especially the youth — our young people. I see the ribbon skirts and the shirts, and I am so proud, not just because it mimics our traditional clothing, but because we are proud of who we are. For so long, the European people wanted us to be ashamed of who we are. We are a walking love letter to our community, our Nation, the Lenape.

This trip is for you, the youth, so that you can pass these stories to your children and their children. We are all born embedded into the land —there are thousands of stories waiting to be told that come from the land. All that we need is found from within.

This trip may not seem as important to you right now, but you will know the importance as you get older. Our home is here in the United States, and we have made a new home in Canada, but we must not forget the sacrifices and lives lost to make our home stand so that we are safe. This particular area I am standing on is the village where our ancestors lie, where our children once played, where the women took care of their families, and where the men hunted and provided for their families. We were in the middle of transitioning to a different life — an unknown life. Life with missionaries, and following a Christian way of life. We were learning how to walk in both worlds. This particular village wasn't given that opportunity — their lives were taken from them. This was the end of their journey in the physical space.

As we lay down the tobacco on their burial grounds, may we let them know that it is okay to rest, because we are here. We have survived, we are healing, and we remember their sacrifice. We will continue to speak the language, and we will raise our children up to know their history, and the ancestors that have come before them. We are a living, walking love letter to the souls here today — that they can rest peacefully because we are here.

May we continue to build communities that are healthy, loving, and strong as we carry our ancestors' voices forward, as a love letter to our future generations.

Anushiik Kiishulumukweengu el-miilyengu yoon kway kiishwihk, thank you Creator for giving us this day, *mech giish daaptoneh,* I am done talking, *anushiik,* thank you.

About the Author

A fanatic of all things dark and creepy, Neil Sater lives with his wife, Mary, in the Cleveland, Ohio area. They have two grown children and two grandchildren. Having spent his career doing other things, Neil is happy to be now finding time for writing. He has published three supernatural mysteries. Neil's debut novel, *Phantom Realm: The Haunting of Misery Mansion*, and his latest novel, *Atrocity: The Haunting of Moravian Village,* both earned the #1 New Release rating in YA Ghost Stories. Neil's second book, *Mercy Killing: The Haunting of Ghoul House,* became a Supernatural Mysteries bestseller. A Horror Writers Association member, Neil is currently working on his next supernatural mystery (like his other books, also set in Homer County, Ohio), which will be published in 2026.

Follow Neil Sater, author on Facebook:

https://www.facebook.com/AuthorSater/

Follow Neil Sater, author on Amazon:

https://www.amazon.com/author/sater

Sign up for Neil Sater's newsletter through his website:

https://authorsater.com/

Printed in Dunstable, United Kingdom

64853943R00153